Table of contents

Cover design by {Donald Derek Dalton}

Visit {state-of the-art.com}

Book design by {Brian K. Paschall}

Visit my website at {brianpaschall.com}

Printed in the {United States of America}

Third Printing: {2023} {Brian K. Paschall}

Aleahcym

Origins

Brian Keith Paschall

Special thanks

I want to take this opportunity to thank God for what he does and provides in my life, my wife and children for being supportive of me. Donna Jennings (mom 2) for taking time out of her life to read and red mark my rough draft. I would like to thank Derek Dalton for the awesome book cover; your art work is amazing. Thank you to all the people close to me for your encouragement. Special Thanks to my friend Isaac. An extra special thanks to you the reader, for taking time out of your lives to read this story.

Chapter One

The beginning

naktuvuk Pass, Alaska, many years ago, along the banks of the Anaktuvuk River, two tribes have co-existed for generations. One tribe is known as the Hunters, and the other as the Fishers. They are known as the Nunamiut to the outside world, which means "People of the Land." Although they live as separate tribes, they work together to have lived in peace and harmony.

One evening, just as it was getting dark, an elder of the Hunters tribe lay sick in his bungalow. He calls for all the elders of both tribes to come to his hut so that he may share with them a prophetic vision that he has received. Everyone gathered around his bed. He reaches out for a bronze cup that contains fresh drinking water mixed with myrrh to help with his pain. After a sip, he begins to speak slowly." The Darkness is coming to consume you all; fear not." He gasps for a new breath of air and coughs up a lump of blood. Then, the closest one to him wipes his mouth with an old garment and says to him, "Continue, sir" as he regains his composure, he speaks again." She conceived in darkness; is she which holds the light." He tries to catch his breath with these words, but no more air can he take into his lungs, and he passes away; they all begin to whisper amongst themselves, wondering what this means.

It was a brisk early fall morning. Just before sunrise, Asaaluk stretched out across her bed made of straw and fresh grass. She climbs out of bed feeling full of life and good cheer; today is Asaaluk's fifteenth birthday, and she is

excited to find out what the secret is finally? Today, the

tribes' women will take her and celebrate her

transformation into adulthood and share the secret with her.

Now, you would think that at least one fifteen-year-old girl

would come back and share with the other children what

the secret is, but it has never happened. Not even once.

Some would say that when they come back, they are

different. Like adult grown-up different. Not in how they

look but in how they would act. When a female child turns

thirteen, she is responsible for caring for and watching over

the younger children at night, so the adults in the tribe can

go out and hunt. At fifteen, your responsibility changes

from watching children to joining the hunt. Most teenagers

assume that this is what the secret is.

But for Asaaluk, she would know by the end of the

day. Asaaluk went through most of her day walking around

the village, gathering herbs for her parents, and doing her

chores. She only has one task left to finish, gathering firewood. It was starting to get late, so she went out to the edge of the village and began getting what she could carry in her cart. The sun is fading fast, so she starts her long walk down the cut trail back toward the village when she notices a strange odor in the air. The stronger the scent gets, the more fearful and weary she becomes. She tries to rationalize away her feelings as just being paranoid. The sun is now dropping below the horizon, so the visibility is just at that right time of day, where the light and darkness meet in the distance, and your eyes can play tricks on you. In the distance, she can see the dull orange glow of a warm fire burning. She slowly starts to make her way toward it, pulling her cart behind her. As she approaches the fire, she lifts her head to the sky. She glances up, gazes at the stars overhead, and then sniffs the air.

This time the smell is almost overpowering, and it terrifies her.

She drops the cart handle beside the fire, burning just outside of a hut. She knows this place; it belongs to Alec, the Chief Elder of the Fisher's tribe. His wife had given birth to twin boys the day before. Asaaluk listens for a moment. Then she hears horrifying screams, along with loud growls and the sound of babies crying. She runs to the hut as fast as possible and throws back the caribou skin door. She sees a giant polar bear mauling one of the newborn twins. Marie (Alec's wife) has also been attacked and is already in shock. She is drifting in and out of consciousness, and she has already lost a lot of blood.

Asaaluk is overcome with intense fear and stress as adrenaline surges through her body. She loses all control of her emotions. Then it happens. In an instant, she changes into a werewolf. The change came without any warning or power of her own body; At the exact moment that Asaaluk turned into her werewolf form, every female in her tribe (The Hunter's tribe) could see through her eyes. This sense is part of a werewolf's fight or flight, and werewolves most always choose to fight. This instinct helps them determine how much of the pack is needed for each battle. On this day, they are all come running to aid in this fight. They quickly turn into their wolf forms and race to help young Asaaluk fight off the polar bear.

By the time they arrive, it is too late. Asaaluk has fended off the bear and is in the transition to becoming human again. Marie wakes up and sees Asaaluk in her wolf form during the transition. Kane, the chief elder of Hunter's tribe, notices that Marie is awake and quickly wraps a wolf skin garment around Asaaluk and ushers her out of the hut. The other members of the tribe tend to Marie's wounds. They cannot get the bleeding to stop, so they try to make her comfortable. When Asaaluk gets back to her camp, Kane prepares her a drink to help her get relaxed and to calm her down. Once she is calm, he tells her," I'm sorry you had to find out this way, and I'm sorry I have to do this to you," he said. "What,do what?" she replies. He holds out his hand and shows her. Inside of his hand lays a tiny shiny, silver barbed bit. Before she can even ask what it is, the drink he gave her has taken effect, and she is asleep. He quickly takes a pair of what resembles a metal crimping device and then places the silver barbed bit inside the machine. He clamps it onto Asaaluk's ear, pressing the silver bit deep inside her earlobe. Kane knows that silver embedded under the skin will stop new werewolves from being able to turn. It is this action that teaches them control. After lots of practice, their bodies and minds will overcome the silver, and they will be able to change at will and not out of fear and anger. It's the way things have been since the beginning, and it's this practice that the folklore and legends of the silver bullet were born.

Alec (Chief of the Fishers) returns home from a long day of fishing with his tribesman and is distraught and enraged to find one of his sons is dead, and his wife is barely alive. Everyone exits the hut to give Alec a few moments alone with his dying wife. Marie tells Alec that Asaaluk came into their place dressed as a wolf and that she had attacked and then killed their son. Marie knows that she is dying and won't be around to help raise their surviving son, Enoch. She says to Alec." Make sure that you don't forget about little Alec JR or me." Then in a final last breath, she tells him goodbye and that she loves him. Alec is furious and orders a group to go and collect Asaaluk at once. Alec's clan doesn't waste any time, and they quickly find her asleep inside her hut. They savagely beat her and don't stop until she confesses to a murder she didn't commit.

Alec calls for a meeting at the village square, where

Asaaluk is on trial. Her face is swollen and black and blue

from her beating. Alec wants her put to death for her

alleged crime, but Kane won't have it. He is furious and

defends her, claiming there is no proof of this; he reminds

Alec that she is only a fifteen-year-old child, and all the

evidence points to something different or someone else.

Kane knows that she is innocent, but since Maria singled

her out and with Asaaluk's so-called confession, there is

nothing else that Kane can say or do. Asaaluk remains

silent. Because she is afraid, their secret will be exposed.

Alec talks among his people, and a solution is reached.

Asaaluk will be exiled to Eagle's Cove until the day of her

eighteenth birthday. She will only be allowed to have one

visitor per day. This visitor is only to bring her food and

drink. They are not allowed to speak to her. Eagle's Cove is

a small cave at the top of the mountain. Once inside the

cave, you can see above the clouds surrounding the top of

the mountain. Eagle's cove, under normal circumstances, is a beautiful and peaceful place, but for Asaaluk, it will become a prison of torment and hell. Alec demanded that she be marked with a brand fashioned to suit her crime upon her release as part of her punishment. The brand will be a quarter-sized circle with the letters "MNYAMA" set inside it, meaning BEAST. Asaaluk will not be the only person to receive this mark. Every female of her entire bloodline at birth from this day forward will also receive it. Her tribe will no longer be known as part of the Nunamiut. Her tribe will now be called "Damu Ya Mbwa Mwitu," which means" Pack of wolves." Kane knows that Asaaluk is innocent, but he does not want their secret to be exposed, so he agrees to all the terms; they escort Asaaluk to the cave.

Chapter Two

Asaaluk's Prison

Asaaluk is visited every morning by Kane, who brings her food and water. His stay isn't long, just long enough to check up on her so that he doesn't violate the terms of the agreement. Kane is a strong man of honor and integrity. He feels remorse for Asaaluk being in prison, and each visit fills him with extreme sadness. After about three months into her imprisonment, Kane came to the cave entrance early one morning. He called for Asaaluk, but she refused to go and greet him. He knew something was very wrong but wasn't sure what.

He reaches through the wooded bars and leaves her food and water on the floor. She slowly crawls her way closer toward the cave entrance, barely being able to see through her black and blue, swollen eyes. When he saw how badly she was beaten. Kane was enraged that she couldn't even open her own eyes. Kane opens the bars and enters the cave, takes out his knife, and cuts her bound hands free from the ropes. He wraps his arms around her and whispers, "sorry," she replies with a very humble voice, "this is not your fault." Kane exits the cave; he closes the door and stops, looking very upset; he turns back, facing the entrance, then pulls the wooden barred door off the frame. He looks over at Asaaluk and says, "caves don't need doors; where does he think your gonna go anyway. I will see you tomorrow". Kane makes his way back down the treacherous mountain and back to his village. There he found his wife Emma and explained Asaaluk's condition. Emma is very upset about how Asaaluk was being treated but reminds Kane that there is nothing they can do without starting a war between the two tribes. Skylar, a young female daughter of James and Sky, was eavesdropping on their conversation.

She decided to help; Asaaluk would always take the time out of her life to watch and play with her and was always there for her when she needed a friend. Skylar, a brilliant little girl, knew that her father would go fishing two nights a week, and her mother would be out on the hunt. She always thought it was strange that all the dads fished while all the moms went on the hunt, but she thought this was how things worked. She knew this would be the best opportunity for her to slip away unnoticed, so she waited; just as the moon began to rise, anxiety and even fear filled her spirit, but she determined that she was going, and nothing would stop her. Finally, her hour has come, and she sneaks out and slips unnoticed into the forest and then follows the path to the bottom of the mountain. She makes the treacherous journey to the top of the mountain without incident, and she stands in front of the cave entrance, "Asaaluk, hey, it's me, Skylar. Are you in here?" she said. "Oh my gosh, Skylar, what are you doing here?" Asaaluk replied. "I come to save you from the bad man who hurt you," she said in a troubled voice as tears filled her eyes. Asaaluk throws her arms around her and squeezes her tightly. "It's not safe for you to be here; he could be on his way up the mountain now," Asaaluk said. "That's why we need to hurry!" Skylar exclaims with a loud whisper. " Oh, sweetheart, I know you don't understand, but I can't leave with you," Asaaluk told her while taking her thumb and wiping the tears from Skylar's eyes. "Now, you need to get back home before your daddy sends out a search party; the hunt will be over soon, so you don't have much time," She said. Skylar's eyes got as big as saucers, and she asked," How did you know?"

Asaaluk chuckled, gave a brief but big smile, and said," I was twelve once too and knew when I could sneak out and not get caught. You need to get back," she said.

Skylar reluctantly leaves and returns to her village, sneaks back into her hut without getting caught. So it goes on for months. One night while Skylar was at the cave with Asaaluk, they heard Alec singing while in a drunken state of being, his speech very slurred and cursing every other breath. "Skylar, you need to hide, NOW!" Asaaluk exclaimed. Skylar quickly moves to the back of the cave, where she finds a crack in the cave wall, it's a small crack, but she manages to squeeze into the gap, which opens up to an enormous cavern. Scared that Alec might catch her, she lays down on the cave floor and watches through the crack in the wall as time passes. She even holds her breath so as not to make a sound.

Alec staggers into the cave entrance with his torch in hand, "I thought I heard voices," he yells out. "No, sir, I was singing," Asaaluk responded. He laughs, mocking her by saying," singing, what do you have to sing about?" Then he tosses the torch and backhands her across the face. Then he untied the rope from around his waist, shoved her to the ground, forcefully bound her hand together, and beat her.

The flickering light from the torch reflected the fear in Skylar's eye's as she watched in horror as Alec tore off Asaaluk's garments and forced himself upon her, cursing the entire time he beat and raped her. Skylar was upset, afraid, and angry, but she never made a sound, not even a whimper. Finally, when this horrendous act was over, he cut her hands free, kicked her in the stomach, and left the cave.

Skylar wiggles her way back through the crack and creeps across the cave floor, covers Asaaluk up with her clothing from off the ground, and holds her tightly, sobbing. Then Skylar's feelings turn from tears of sorrow to tears of hate and rage. Her heart races, sweat pours down her forehead, prickles of hair pepper up her arms like dots of rain over an open pond; her eyes begin to reflect the low glow of the torchlight. "shh, calm down, baby, it's all OK, it's all going to be fine" said Asaaluk, trying to stop the change.

It is too late. Suddenly like a roar of thunder, Skylar lets a low but very intimidating growl, then bolts out the cave entrance; having Alec in her sights, she lunges off all fours thrusting herself into Alec, knocking him off the side of the mountain. Alec goes tumbling off the mountainside, while Skylar manages to make a solid landing, and without missing a beat, she sprints down the mountainside and runs to her village. Her parents are waiting for her as she enters the village; she stops running and morphs back into a human; her mother quickly grabs her up and hugs her, then usher her back to their hut, "You shouldn't have gone there. "you need to come inside there is a lot we need to talk about."Sky pours her heart out to Skylar. She reveals everything to her. She is a lycanthrope, and the werewolf gene is passed down only to the females in the tribe. She tells her of the special bond between a mother and daughter.

She explains mothers and daughters can share thoughts and feelings while the baby is in the womb. Sky tells her that she already knows that the pack is connected, and they can see through the eyes of a pack member in danger or scared. Skylar and Sky talk about it all night long. Once she tells her everything, James gives Skylar a cup and says, "here,drink up." It doesn't take long for Skylar to fall asleep, and James implants the bit into her earlobe.

The following day Kane is up early, fixing to make his trip up the mountain to take Asaaluk, her daily food ration. Emma comes running out of their hut, holding some of her old garments, "take these. I feel she will need them," Emma said. She then kisses her husband goodbye, and he goes off to Eagles Cove. Once at the cave entrance, he finds Asaaluk bloodied, busied, and almost naked. Kane gives her the garments from his wife Emma, " I'm so sorry for this," he said. She cracks a half-smile and says to him, " this is not your fault, Kane. You're a good man."

Kane turns and exits the cave, "I'll be back in the morning," he says. Then he starts down the mountain. While on his way down the narrow pathway, sounds of moans reach his ears. Kane stops and listens for a bit, then peers over the edge of the mountainside, where he sees Alec in a pool of blood lying on the top of some rocks below. Kane turns back to the pathway and continues on his way, but being the man he is, he could not do it, so he turns back to help Alec. Kane returns Alec to his village, and his people tend to his wounds and broken bones. Alec claims no recollection of anything that happened, and he doesn't remember going to the cove last night. With Alec's current conditions in mind, they know it will be a long while before he goes anywhere. Skylar continued her visits for months until Alec healed and began going back up to the cove

again. His visits became more frequent and his attacks

more brutal.

Chapter Three

The Ceremony

One thousand, one hundred, and ninety-four painful, agonizing days of being tortured, beat, and raped, have finally passed. Asaaluk has survived two miscarriages and is now with a child again. She will finally be released tonight, as agreed, after her branding ceremony.

Alec is at the center of the village, stoking a pretty good size fire. He is making sure he gets the branding iron cherry red for Asaaluk and enjoys every second of it. Several members of Alec's tribe have suggested that he should just let it go. They feel that Asaaluk has served her time and suffered enough. Alec spits at them and then reminds them that it wasn't their son or wife that she brutally killed.

Everyone from both tribes has gathered at the center of the village.

They are all muttering amongst themselves, and everyone has an opinion on how they should proceed. Finally, Asaaluk is brought to the center of the crowd with her hands bound. She stands before Alec, and all the tribe's people as a dreadful silence falls over the group; they are shocked to see that Asaaluk is pregnant. A child's scream breaks the silence. It's Enoch; he is frantically trying to get Alec to stop. Alec reaches toward the fire and takes out the branding iron, but before anyone can stop him, he forcibly grabs Asaaluk by the hair of her head and shoves it over to the side, placing the branding iron below her left ear. He burns the mark into her skin while cursing and laughing at her.

Asaaluk doesn't even flinch or make a sound. Kane runs to her and frees her from the restraints when it is over. Asaaluk steps forward and gets into Alec's face, nose to nose. She smiles savagely and says." enjoy your happiness while you can, for it will be short-lived," then she walks away.

Being the pack leader, Kane's wife, Emma has the strength of ten men. she quickly overtakes Alec and takes the branding iron away from him. She puts the iron back into the coals and begins to heat it again. Then, she calls for all the females of her tribe to step closer to the fire. As they step forward, Emma says," This we do to honor Asaaluk, who Alec falsely accused and imprisoned. Alec has mistreated her. He has beaten and raped her while you were responsible for her."

Emma then takes the hot iron and brands herself just below her left ear, and passes it to the next pack member in the line. Every female in the tribe takes Asaaluk's mark and bares the pain with her. Emma looks towards two of her most vital women in the pack, and without having to say a single word, they restrain Alec. Alec struggles, but he is no match for two werewolves even in their human form."YOU," Emma says to Alec, " you've done these things to her in vain. She is innocent of killing your wife and son, but you're not innocent, and your crimes shall not go unpunished." Emma takes the branding iron and turns it so that the brand will read upside down. "Killing you would be too easy," she said, and she placed the hot iron on Alec's forehead; unforgivably, she used excessive force, branding him down to the bone. Emma tells Alec, " even after your death, after the worms have eaten off all your flesh, your mark will remain, not only in this life but even the next, and I will hunt you down and erase you from existence." In shock from the pain, Alec's skin goes from a dark brown to a very pale white. He collapses to the ground at Emma's feet. It doesn't take long for him to regain consciousness and his color. He jumps to his feet and escapes into the night. Emma feels that something isn't right. It seemed odd that his skin went as pale white as it did, even with the pain. She quickly brushes the thoughts away and decides she just imagined it and didn't give it a second thought. Kane, Emma, and all hunter's tribes permanently choose to leave the fishers. They want to make new village miles downriver. They want to live in peace and be away from Alec.

When Alec returns to his tribe, he explains that it's time to teach their children in the old ways. He tells them they all must revert to the old way of doing things. They must learn to do everything as their ancestors did. Because he fears war is coming and they must all get prepared.

The first few weeks after the two tribes went their separate

ways were brutal. After all, each tribe had grown

accustomed to having the other to help out. It meant extra

work for everyone, but they slowly got used to doing it

themselves. The hunter's tribe, not realizing how angry

Alec was or what he could do, assumed all was over and

relaxed. They went about life as usual. The fisher's tribe, on

the other hand, was preparing hard for what they thought

would eventually come, war.

Chapter Four

The Baby

I t was a frigid night when Assluk went into labor.
Kane and Emma were present, as were the rest of the
members of her tribe. They felt an urgency to protect
mother and child from an attack they felt might come. It
was not an easy delivery for eighteen-year-old Asaaluk.
She had already been in labor for forty-eight hours and was
exhausted. Emma told her to push just one last time, and
she finally heard her baby cry for the first time. At the same
time, a female tribe member outside spotted what she
thought was a polar bear close to the tent. She reported it to
Kane, who sent a few members out to see what they could
find; as the pack got close, they followed the footprints of
the polar bear, which led to a small stream, but on the other
side of the stream, there was only human tracks, and

nothing else. They decided that the bear must have come close because of the noise. Kane and Emma were nervous to hear about the bear, and they agreed that they must be very cautious for the next few days, but the attack they feared didn't come.

Asaaluk fell in love with her child, a girl she named Danotta. Asaaluk decided then and there that she would do whatever it took to keep her child safe. She worried that Alec might try and take her child. She also hoped that Danotta wouldn't ask any questions about her father because she had no intention of telling her. The only thing that she wanted her daughter to know was how much she loved her and how to defend herself when the time came.

Danotta was the first female born after Asaaluk's release. She was the first infant marked shortly after birth. The entire tribe was present that night; they had deemed the mark sacred. It will pass it down to all generations of the tribe's females.

Danotta grows into a beautiful child. She is quiet and mostly keeps to herself. Her mother never told her about her father, and she has never wondered where he was. She knew that her family was different. The other children her age had both parents, but this was normal for her, and her mother had enough love for her, and she wasn't missing out on anything. One of Danotta's favorite pass times was exploring and living here; she had many opportunities. Alaska can be very dangerous for a little girl, but Danotta was never afraid. Her favorite place to explore was Eagle's Cove. It is peaceful there, and she loved to sit and think and watch the polar bears in the distance down in the valley. However, there was one polar bear that drew her interest.

Even at that distance, it seemed that it was always watching her.

One morning she got up very early. She wanted to go to her favorite spot and think; she kissed her mother goodbye, and off she went. Asaaluk didn't like the idea of her eleven-year-old child running off. Still, she knew that Danotta needed to find herself and her wolf self, so she allowed her some freedoms, and besides that, Asaaluk knew her wolf instinct would alarm her of any life-threatening dangers. She didn't realize that Danotta was meeting up with two children from the other tribe all this time, and the three children had become relatively close friends. Danotta makes her long hike to the cove. When she arrives at the bottom of the mountain, her two friends greet her, Eric and Donovan. Donovan is about three years older than Danotta, while Eric is much older, Danotta instinctively knows that her mother would disapprove, but she isn't entirely sure why. At this point in her young life, she hasn't ever done anything that she knew her mother would disapprove of, but she can't help it. She feels drawn to the boys, almost as if she has known them forever.

The trio does the climb to the top of the mountain. Once there, Danotta, Eric, and Donovan sit and talk, Sometimes chucking a rock over the side to see who can throw it the furthest. Eric picks up a flat rock and tosses it out of the cave entrance; the cave floor is wet and slippery, and he loses his footing and falls on his bum. Donovan and Danotta laugh; Eric, finding it funny also, laughs along with them. Danotta picks up a rock, takes a few steps forward, pulls her throwing arm in toward her, and thrusts the rock forward with so much force she skids to the edge of the cave, flapping her arms like a bird for balance so that she doesn't fall over the edge. Still, it isn't enough. Donovan could see the look of fear and panic in her eyes, but he was too late, and over the ledge, she went. Donovan shadow shifted and quickly moved across the ground and down the cliff face at what would seem like light speed; he caught up with Danotta while she was in mid-fall. He shifts from a shadow to a giant bird, grabbing Danotta by an arm and a leg, and then swoops down to the earth. He lets her go, and she hits the ground with a thump. The landing knocks the breath out of her, but she is not hurt. Donovan quickly shifts back to human form and runs to her and hugs her, wondering if she is OK.

Embraced in the arms of Donovan, Danotta is in a state of shock and extremely frightened, and when it happens. She begins to shake uncontrollably, all the hairs on her body become thick and prickly and stand on end, and then, She makes the change into her werewolf form. Donovan continues to hold and whisper into her ear, "it's OK, sister, your safe now, please calm down, just calm down." Danotta returns to human form, and almost as quickly as everything happened, it was over. In polar bear form, Eric finally makes his way down the mountain and proceeds over to them. He shifts into human form in front of Danotta and says," Well, I guess the secret is out, and it looks like we found ourselves a little wolfie girl; what do you think Knock, Knock" said Eric; I told you not to call me that replied Donovan!" " I guess your father will be very proud of you, well, I mean, us," Eric said. "No, Eric, my father will not ever find out about this," He said. " Enoch Donovan Horn, I intend to see that he does; this is what he has been training us for since birth." Eric said."

Eric, you're right," said Enoch. Looking in Danotta's direction, he said, " sorry for this." Enoch shifts into an exact copy of Danotta's wolf form and slashes Eric's throat. He yells to Danotta, "run! Run fast and don't come back; you're not safe here!". Danotta, confused, takes off, running as fast as she can. Enoch (Donovan) shifts back to human and opens his hand to the wind. The wind catches a strand of Danotta's hair that he's been holding and blows it off his hand. He sadly watches it fly away. When Enoch returns home, he informs his dad that there was a werewolf attack and Eric had been killed, and he explains that he only survived by running away. Enoch is viewed as a coward and Eric as a hero from this day forward.

Danotta was running fast as she could to make her way home. As she is franticly crying, she wraps her arms around her mother. Asaaluk comforts her, telling her it is going to be alright. Asaaluk has been preparing to soothe Danotta because she knew her daughter had almost been killed from her fall today. Asaaluk didn't realize that Danotta wasn't upset about the fall, she was upset about Donovan and Eric, but she knew she couldn't let her mother know that. But Asalluk already knew.

Back at Enoch's village, Alec, Enoch's father, was extremely hard on Enoch (Donovan), constantly reminding him that he was a coward. Alec even told Enoch that not only did Eric die, but he was also dead to him, that Eric might as well have been his natural son, and that Enoch was nothing more than a grunt to him, just another expendable soldier on the field.

Enoch was brilliant. He took his father's abuse and never went against him face to face and began raising an army behind his father's back as he got older. He already had many followers. They were from both races of shifters, shadow, and shapeshifters, that had secretly informed Enoch of the truth about his father. But, Enoch had a dream of one dominant race. A race like him, who can both shape and shadow shift, and one day co-exist with the wolves, and he is just waiting for the right time to leave and prove his father wrong.

After Danotta's first change, her mother began explaining to her about her werewolf heritage. The silver bit would have to be put in her ear to help her learn to control the change. She would be able to change at will and not out of fear once she learned to overcome the silver. Danotta understood that it would take her lots of practice to control her changes, and she spent every day trying to learn how to do just that.

It was hard for Danotta at first. There were times that Danotta didn't think she would ever learn to change independently. She even tried to put herself in situations that would cause her to turn, but nothing worked. Then, out of the blue, one day, while Danotta was out by herself, she thought about her lost friends. She has tried hard the last few months not to think about them. She is so caught up in her thoughts that she walks to their old meeting spot without realizing it. An immediate wave of grief overcomes her, and suddenly, without any warning, it happens. The thing that she has been trying so hard to do for months, she makes the change.

It was so sudden and unexpected that it surprised and excited her at the same time. She races home to tell her mother. Back at the village, Asaaluk was waiting on her to return. She is happy that Danottta is learning to overcome the silver bit inside her earlobe. Suddenly Danotta could sense something was wrong," what's troubling you"? she asked. Asaaluk smiles and replies," It's nothing; I've just been having some weird dreams lately," she said. Danotta exclaims, "The Darkness!!" Asaaluk's face went from a smile to concern when Danotta said that. Then, in a concerned, scared tone, Asaaluk said," tell me your dreams and do not leave out any details!" OK, Mom, but it is just a dream. My dream started with a dull orange glow off in the distance, so I began to walk towards it, and when I got close enough, I could see you. You were scared like I'd never seen you before. And you were as your wolf; you were fighting the Dragon called Darkness. I could not see the Dragon, not even through your eyes.

Then from out of nowhere appeared the Dragon and it attacked you, not with fire, but with darkness and when the darkness surrounded you, I could no longer remember you, it was like I never knew you, I had no feelings for you, no sense of loss, It was like I never knew you existed. Then a little girl appeared to me ." "Aleahcym!", Asaaluk interrupted. "Yeah! how did you know her name?" Danotta exclaimed! "Because in my dream, after the darkness struck me and I was in the void, she came to me to assure me that it would all be OK. Remember that there is light in the darkness, said Asaaluk. "Is this part of our bond that we can share dreams?" asked Danotta. "I don't know," she replied.

As time passes, they both talk about the dream less and less, until eventually, it's just a distant memory.

After a few years have passed, Danotta is blossoming into adulthood and has learned to control her change. She can turn at will any time she feels that it is necessary. She still spends a great deal of time at Eagle's Cove. It is still an extraordinary place for her. She still misses her friends but has put that behind her. One fateful day while she is there, she meets Marc. Marc is a kind of a geeky-looking guy who has a great big heart. He is a climatologist in Alaska on business, making changes to some weather equipment near Eagle's Cove. Danotta fell in love almost instantly with Marc, and the two of them would spend lots of time together. Every day for months, Danotta would invite Marc back to the village to have dinner with her and her mother.

The tribe did not like that there was an outsider in the village. It took some time, but they grew to like him. Marc was just a likable, friendly, goofy guy with whom Danotta was madly in love. Everyone could tell Marc loved Danotta. After Marc completed his work, he would find reasons not to leave, but after a while, his supervisor would finally say to him that it was time to come back to New York. Marc knew that it was inevitable. He could not stall on his boss any longer. When he had to leave to go back home, Danotta decided to leave with him. She couldn't stand the thoughts of losing him. So she goes back to her tribe to inform her mother, she packed what little belongings she has, and she leaves with Marc for New York City.

New York is an entirely different world for her. It is a place where she doesn't fit in at all. There is never the need to hunt for her food or cook over an open flame. In an instant, all the aspects of her life that she knew had changed to the extremes. She loves all the lights and buildings, but she fears keeping her secret will be difficult. She knows that she cannot tell Marc about her tribe's secret. After a few months, Marc suspects that she isn't happy and brings Danotta back to visit her village. She is excited to be going home. She misses her mother, her tribe, and Eagles Cove. This visit is also very special to Marc because he plans to ask Asaaluk, in secret, for her permission to marry her daughter. Once back in Alaska, after all the hellos and hugging have passed, Marc follows Asaaluk outside to help bring in more wood for the fire. While outside, he is very nervous. The palms of his hands are sweating, and he wipes them on his kakis, then proceeds to ask Asaaluk if he could marry her daughter. Asaaluk gives him her blessing, but her blessing comes with a warning to Marc's surprise. She tells Marc, "if she accepts your proposal, there is a truth you will need to know. If you accept the truth, all will be well, but if not, all could be lost." Marc is confused, but he agrees.

That night Kane called a village meeting. Every tribe member came together at the village center and grouped up around the fire. Kane calls everyone to order, and things quickly quiet down. Marc takes Danotta's hand, kneels before her, and asks, "will you be my wife." Her eyes filled up with tears, and she wrapped her arms around his neck, saying, "I will, "but we need to talk first," Danotta said. Kane and all the other husbands welcome Marc as a member of their family and tribe. "Marc," Kane says, "as a member of this family, there is something you need to know," A secret that goes back to the ancients. You will be the first outsider we will trust with our secret." But, "your life depends on you keeping it a secret, "said Kane. Some of the men chuckle in the background. "Men show him," said Kane. The men stop giggling and remove the upper part of their garments, revealing to Marc the upper torsos of their bodies and some of their backs. Marc was at a loss for words; at what he saw, all the men had very large deep scaring on them. The scaring looks a lot like claw marks left by something big. Finally, Marc asks," Do I have to fight a bear in a meek voice?" Everybody starts laughing; Dougie, standing next to Marc, puts his arms around Marc and Danotta, laughing and saying, " this guy will fit in just fine."

Kane, with a smile, says," Marc, every woman of this tribe, or should I say pack, leaves her unique mark, and Danotta will be no different." Marc, at this point, is perplexed and scared as hell, but he truly loves Danotta with all his heart. So Marc removes his shirt and says to Kane, " OK do it beat me, hit me, do what you have to because I love Danotta, and if this is what I have to do, I will do it," said Marc.

Kane replies," Nobody will beat you; it's not like what you think, and remember you ask for it, ladies," said Kane. Before Marc could even blink an eye in a flash, all the females in Danotta's tribe changed and showed Marc their secret. Marc show's no fear but is astonished at what he is witnessing. Danotta, in her werewolf form, makes her way to Marc, snarling and growling. She gets up in Marc's face, but Marc doesn't show any fear; instead, he wraps his arms around her and whispers," I love you, Danotta, no matter what, I love you." Danotta changes back and kisses Marc on the lips. Kane shouts, "let's go have a wedding!." "Wait," said Marc, "what did you change your mind," asked Kane? " Hell no, but I didn't get my scars." Kane laughs and smacks Marc on the back and says, "Marc, my boy, you will earn those stripes the first time you mate," Marc blushes. Marc and Danotta were married in the village that night, and everything is explained to Marc that the werewolf gene was dormant in the males. Only the females could change, and female werewolves mark their mates to show ownership and serve as a warning to other female werewolves in their tribe or others to stay away.

Marc quits his job, and they decide to live in the village. Marc is the first-ever outsider to be accepted into the tribe; he begins to learn their ways.

He swiftly learned their ways. Kane and Marc became very close friends. Kane taught him how to hunt, track, fish, and fight. Kane's motto was to defend your family and remember we are all family. Marc, a reasonably wealthy man, brought more non-traditional methods, like riffles. Kane, Emma, and Asaaluk would teach Marc how to hunt with the pack and how the group would use the male's scent as a way to move the game out of the forest and into open fields where the ladies would take down their prey, and Marc would teach Kane how to hunt with a rifle.

Much time has passed, and Marc and Danotta now have three children, Marla, Michael, and Aaluk. Aaluk is named for Danotta's mother Asaaluk. One night, the children were finishing up their chores. One of them noticed a shadow off in the distance. They strain their eyes, trying to see what it could have been, but at a second glance, it was gone. A few minutes later, there is a loud war cry, and it comes from the direction of Kane's hut. Danotta and two pack members quickly changed into werewolf form and raced off toward Kane's place. Kane is fighting off a polar bear; it has dragged him out of his hut and severely mauled him. This is no ordinary polar bear; on its head is a mark where no hair has grown; it is a circle with the upside-down letters (AMAYNM). The entire pack attack and finally kill the bear. Upon the bear's death, it turns back into its proper form, it is Alec, and Alec has killed Kane. Emma approaches Kane's body and completely freaks out; she turns into her wolf form and then rips into Alec's lifeless body. His body shredded into pieces within a minute. When she returns to her human form and is very troubled, she asks the pack to burn both bodies. She is exhausted, so she goes into her hut to morn, as the entire pack morns her loss with her.

The following day everyone begins to put the pieces together. Alec killed his wife and son all those years ago because his son didn't have the shape-shifting gene. He was always rather fond of Asaaluk; he had waited until she was close enough to his tent so she would hear the attack and he could frame her for the murders in front of the village people. Alec had her thrown into the cave, so her could do with her as he pleased with her. Alec figured out their secret, and he knew that Kane would embed a silver bit into her skin to keep her from making the change to keep their secret safe.

Danotta was shocked to see this dead shapeshifter on the ground wearing her mother's mark upside down on his forehead; This is one story that Danotta had not heard. She has no idea that the monster she just helped rip apart was her father. Danotta knew that her mother was a courageous woman and well respected. She also knew that the mark was to honor her mother, but Danotta didn't know why. So the first thing she decides is that it is time to start asking some questions.

Danotta sits down with her mother and begins to ask questions, one right after the other. Asaaluk tells her daughter everything, from the polar bear attack on the twins to being imprisoned at Eagles cove, down to Alec rapping her, and that's how she was conceived. Asaaluk asked her not to tell her children until they were ready to know. Danotta took it all very well, considering all the circumstances, but she is saddened to find out about her father that way. To Danotta, the worst part was finding out that her mother was imprisoned and raped at Eagle's cove because that is her favorite place to go and be alone to think. Danotta returned to her hut when they finished talking and told Marc everything.

Chapter Five

The Death of Innocents and The Birth of a Monster

Meanwhile, Enoch had learned through experimentation that shapeshifters who took injections of his blood got extremely sick and almost died. Still, shadow shifters who took an infusion of his blood can also shapeshift only for short periods; the longest time recorded was two hours.

Enoch and his followers begin to grow. They become a mighty group. Enoch decided that it was time to expand. He sent out his troops to infiltrate the human population and see how ordinary, non-shifting people (humans) would react to being injected with his blood. What they learned astounded him. After testing people of all blood types, people with O-positive blood died almost immediately after the injection. People with other blood types got very sick but didn't die and couldn't shift either. People who received the injection with A Negative blood type (the same type as Enoch) didn't die or get sick and were able to shadow shift. A seventeen-year-old female was the first human who was successfully able to shadow shift. Her name is Asterisk, and Enoch deems her his daughter. Enoch's army has become very strong and successful, establishing members in powerful governments and non-government organization's around the globe. After his father's death, he decides it is time to move forward with his ultimate goal, global domination. Enoch ordered all followers of his father's rule killed, and his motto was "no enemies left, leaves no future regrets." Enoch traveled around the globe for years, recruiting people to his secret society, and in his absence, he left Asterisk in charge. She rules with an iron fist, and her first orders are that every member of Enoch's secret society will take a tattoo (known as asterisk's mark.) The tattoo will be placed in the white part of either eye. This mark represents loyalty and allegiance and her ownership over them. Enoch loves this idea so much that he gives her equal control and names his new society, Asterisk's Army, nicknamed by their enemies as Asterisk's kill squad or A.K.S.

Enoch has become a mighty, wealthy man, with members established in every nation, secret organization, government agency, and major industry worldwide. His goals were simple, infiltrate, gain trust, climb through the ranks, then gain total control, and if that didn't work, kill your way to the top. He and his members are very good at it. He would tell his troops, " Humans are weak and easy, the slightest display of power followed by authority, and they cower before you. They will offer anything for a piece of the power you possess, and then they will either be ruled or killed. "

Enoch had planned to leave the werewolves alone, but his plans have changed since his father's death. So he calls a meeting with his ten heads of power. Enoch is amazed that Asterisk has not aged when they all arrive. Enoch stands before Asterisk, takes his hand, and gently brushes his fingertips across her face," remarkable, absolutely remarkable," he said. Asterisk takes two steps back and says to him, "watch this," she pulls a dagger from the sheath off her belt and places the blade on her throat. Then, with plenty of force, she slashes her throat open, choking on her blood, and falls to the ground at Enoch's feet. Then just before passing out, she shadow shifts.

While in shadow form, she gets back up on her feet, then she shifts back to her human form, completely restored to the way she looked at the time of her life when she received the injection of Enoch's blood. "I have top scientists worldwide trying to figure this out as we speak, but of course, under our complete control, can you imagine an army of indestructible soldiers," she said. "Outstanding, I am well pleased, well pleased indeed. "Now, let's get right to business. It has come to my attention that many of our members seem to fear the werewolf population. We have no reason to believe that the werewolves will be a threat to us or our cause, but some members seem to think I'm weak for not addressing this situation sooner. I have already spoken to the more outspoken members. Unfortunately, they have chosen to leave the organization for reasons unknown (he paused and gave a little chuckle). Their bloodline has been genocide from the face of the Earth, a nasty virus that only targets specific D.N.A. markers. Let me clarify what I say (he draws a symbol on a dry erase board and lays it down on the table). Any wolves bearing this mark will be spared and brought to me personally. I might have some family ties, so be careful not to harm them. Your families can't afford to catch a virus, am I clear? "Good, now, let's close this meeting and have some lunch," he said. (Asterisk, on the other hand, seems to have

her own plans in mind.)

Chapter Six

The Warning

A few days later, a young boy comes into the village. He is from the fishers tribe, and he is screaming for Asaaluk and Danotta at the top of his lungs. They all come running to him," What's wrong," Danotta asked. He takes a few minutes to catch his breath, then he says," my name is Danyon. My father told me to let you know that he is Asaaluk's distant cousin born into the fisher's tribe". He gasped and took another breath, then said."There is trouble. He warned me that Enoch is bringing a war you can't win, and Enoch will take Michael. You won't believe me, but the village is full of shadow and shapeshifters. If they knew I came here to warn you, Enoch would have me killed." he said. At that exact moment, Danyon turned into a dark shadow. The shadow dispersed into a billion tiny shadow dots that shot off like lighting into billion different directions. He was gone. "Oh my Gosh!" Danotta said, "Michael?, why Michael?" she asks. Asaaluk replies "Because Michael could be a shifter also."

Danotta rushes back to tell Marc he must take their children and leave, go to his family in New York, and she will keep in touch by mail. Both in their teens, Marla and Michael are very reluctant about leaving. They want to stay and help fight, then Asaaluk reminds them by saying," Marla, you have not made your first change, and Michael is a male. The werewolf gene is dormant, and he has never shown any signs of being a shadow shifter. There would be nothing here either of you could do, and you need to leave, help protect your younger sister, and Marla, you have to teach her the things that you will soon learn yourself." she said. The next day Marc and his children are on a flight out of Alaska.

Danotta asks Asaaluk," what can we do?" "We have some time. Shadow shifters need complete darkness before they can attack outside the shadow realm, so we still have about a month," said Asaaluk

"Yeah, and then what? The shapeshifters we can take, but shadow shifters are a different story. They can harm us, and we can't touch them." So Danotta said. "we pray," said Asaaluk." remember, if a shadow shifter is caught outside of the shadow realm, during daylight, it is powerless and loses the ability to shift back to human," said Asaaluk.

Marc hates leaving Danotta, but the thought of losing his kids is even worse. Every day he waits for a letter that he isn't sure will ever come, not knowing if there was a battle and if Danotta was still alive. Marc is beside himself and doesn't know what to do. Marc waits, and every day, he checks the P.O box that they had set up, Weeks go by and no word, weeks turn into months, and finally, a letter comes. The letter is to let Marc know to keep the kids in hiding. So far, all is well, and there hasn't been an attack yet. The kids adapt to New York life reasonably well, making friends, and going to school. Marla has learned to change at will and has complete control over her wolf self, and she is trying to teach Aaluk as well.

On the other hand, Michael has put space between himself and his sisters. Marla knows something is wrong but doesn't know what. When Marc checks the mail the next day, there is a letter. It is all typed, even the envelope. Marc's letter reads, If you wish to see Danotta alive again, bring Michael home before the eighteenth. The eighteenth is only three weeks away.

Marc and Michael begin to pack for the trip, and they would have to leave immediately. Marc will leave Marla to watch her sister while they are gone. Marc and Michael had just left for the airport when there was a knock on the Apartment door. "Uh, Who is it'" said Marla hesitantly. At the entrance stands Nathan, a boy who lives down the hall; Nathan and Marla have been friends since they got to New York, "It's Nate, are you guys OK?" he said. Nathan was a sharp-looking, brilliant young man who caught Marla's eye. Marla opened the door, grabbed Nathan, pulled him into the house, and closed and locked the door quickly.

"Yeah, we are good. But unfortunately, we have a family emergency. Dad and Michael had to go out of town for a few days," said Marla. Marla doesn't know that Nathan has had his eye on her for a while now. " My parents are always gone, so I wondered if I could bring over some movies, and we could watch them together," said Nathan insecurely. "I would like that very much," Marla said. "Great! I'll see you in a bit then," said Nathan. Marla thought that this was a great idea. Finally, she has someone to help take her mind off things, and she doesn't have to be alone either. A few weeks have passed, and Marla and Nathan have movie nights a lot. They seemed to have fallen in love. They have still had no word from Marla's dad or brother, but she can feel that they are safe. Today is the eighteenth, and Marla, Nathan, and Aaluk have plans to all make dinner together, watch a movie, and plan to watch the lunar eclipse from the living room window.

Nathan comes over at about 4:30 pm. Marla and Aaluk have made spaghetti for dinner. After they finish eating and then cleaning up, they all sit on the sofa to watch a movie. At around 7:00 pm, Nathan and Marla got very close. Aaluk falls asleep, so Marla carries her to her room and puts her to bed. They spread out a blanket on the floor in front of the window and turned out every light in the apartment so that they could watch the eclipse. Nathan leans into Marla and kisses her for the first time. He is afraid of how she will react. They are both scared, but Marla kisses him back, and soon fear turns to passion, and passion turns to lust, and they begin to make out in front of the window during the eclipse.

At the peak of the eclipse, Marla has a vision. She can see her mother and hear her mother's voice. Her voice sounds covered in fear as she is screaming. Danotta turns into her wolf form, attacking polar bears and trying to attack shadows. Marla sees her dad and brother being chased, then the unthinkable happens. Her dad gets pounded from behind and is killed. Then Asaaluk is attacked and killed, as she is being torn apart by a shadow. Michael loses control and goes blood drunk, trying to kill anything that isn't a wolf. A shadow shifter suddenly attacks him. At that very moment in time, Michael makes the change into a shadow wolf. Michael is the first-ever shadow-shifting werewolf. In this form, he discovers that he can slay shadow shifters. Marla and Nathan continue to make out while she has her vision. Marla turns into her wolf form and marks Nathan as her mate.

Both Nathan and Marla fall unconscious onto the blanket in front of the window. The following day they both wake up before Aaluk gets up. They get dressed, barely speaking to each other. Nathan finally breaks the silence saying, "We should go, you know." "Go where?" said Marla. "Alaska," Nathan replied," I saw everything, your dad, brother, your mom, and strangely I feel like I lost them too." Nathan wrapped his arms around Marla and said, "I love you, Marla, wolf or not, and I know you love me also. You marked me last night," Nathan said. " how do you know all this!" Marla exclaimed. "I don't know. I just do; I saw everything you saw last night. It was like I was looking through your eyes while you were looking through your mom's eyes," said Nathan. "What about your parents?" Marla asked. "My mother took off four months ago, and dad, your guess is as good as mine," said Nathan. "We need to wait before we just take off to Alaska." Michael will be coming home, and there is not much that we can do.

Staying here helps keeps us safe."

Aaluk came into the room. She walks up to Nathan and says," Mommy said welcome to the family"' she then turns to Marla and says," Grandma said you must name her Aleahcym." Name who, Aleahcym?" asked Marla. "She said you would say that and told me to tell you, the child you both just conceived," said Aaluk. Nathan and Marla were both at a loss for words. Finally, Aaluk said, " Mommy and Grandma came to visit me last night while I was sleeping, and Grandma said she would be Aleahcym's spirit guide." Aaluk giggles and runs back into her room, singing," I going be an aunty, an aunty, an aunty."

Even though Marla knew her parents were gone, she didn't feel a sense of loss for them, and it was like she knew they were always going to be close to her, yet she was still saddened, knowing that they would never return home.

Meanwhile, back in Alaska, this battle is over. Most of the shapeshifters have been defeated. Michael slew multitudes of shadow shifters. There was an enormous retreat. Asterisk escapes with her life and a female child. With all commotion, no one seems to notice that she is missing. Michael stays and helps his tribe; they must do the traditional thing and burn their dead. Michael is not feeling very well, and he is drained physically and mentally. Michael fades in and out like he is trying to turn into his shadow wolf form but does not have control over it. Michael goes into the hut and lays down to rest for a while. While Michael is sleeping, all the members of the tribe collect outside his hut, waiting for him to wake up. When Michael wakes up, he feels drained but better; pulling back the caribou skin door, he jumps, surprised to see everyone gathered outside his hut. "Uh, hi," he said confusedly in his soft-spoken voice. Loud muttering is coming from the crowd, and people are bombarding Michael with questions

quicker than he can answer them. Finally, Michael shouts,"
STOP! what on earth is going on with all of you?" "How is
it that you can kill a shadow shifter?" "I'm not sure yet,"
Michael replies. " Pull yourselves together. As I learn
more, you will too. I've got to get back to Marla". Emma
steps to the front of the crowd. She tells her people to go
back to their homes and give Michael some space. She
handed Michael a branding iron and said, "take this with
you. We have fashioned one for each family, and Marla
will need it." "What do you mean Marla will need it?".
"Marla is now with child Michael; Aleahcym was
conceived last night. We all saw it." Michael interrupts "
Aleahcym? you said, just conceived, and she has a name
already?" Michael exclaimed! "Michael, she must be
named Aleahcym. Asaaluk named her, " said Emma. "I
have to get back. I have to keep Marla safe." "by the way,
who is the dad? I need to know whom to torment," said
Michael with a big smile. "Michael, you leave that boy

alone," Emma said. After three days of mourning, Michael packs his belongings, makes the trip to Anchorage, and begins his flight home.

Michael finally arrives home after a two-hour delay, an eight-hour flight, and an hour cab ride. He doesn't even get to open the apartment door before Aaluk screams with excitement, "YEAAAH, Michael is home!" She runs to the door and opens it up. Michael stands in the doorway, half slumped over, and his color is an awful baby powder white. Nathan runs over to him and helps him into the room and over to the sofa where Michael can lay down. "Thank you, Nathan," said Michael. "Dude, how did you know my name?" Nathan said. Michael laughed and said, "well, Nate, I know more than you think." Anything you guy's care to talk about?"Michael asked. "No, nothing, no need to talk about anything uh, huh sounds like everybody already knows," replied Nathan. Aaluk then runs over to the sofa where Michael is, wraps her arms around his neck, and says," It's almost dark; you will feel better then." " And how would you know that, Aaluk?" asked Michael. "Grandma told me," she responded. "Grandma, Oh honey, I'm so sorry Grandma is uh," Michael was interrupted. "Grandma's spirit surrounds us. She talks to me a lot since she has crossed over, as she put it, OH!, and Momma too!" Excitedly Aaluk said. "I know," said Michael.

The sun begins to set on the horizon, and instantly Michael starts to feel better. "how old are you, Nate?" asked Michael. "Funny, you should ask. I turn eighteen tomorrow, as a matter of fact," said Nathan. Then, in a sarcastic voice, Michael asked, " you know Marla is only seventeen, don't you?" Nathan fire's back with a quick response, in the form of a question saying," You do understand that eighteen tomorrow does mean that I was seventeen last night, right? same age as Marla, still a minor", said Nathan. "Well, Nate can you prove that in a court of law?" asked Michael. "No, but I could probably prove that you need a tranquilizer dart every full moon," Nathan says while chuckling. Michael pats Nathan on the back and whispers, "I'm a shadow wolf, can't tranquilize me." He looks over at Marla, smiles, and says, " I like him! can we keep him?" Marla smiled, shaking her head up and down," yes, we can. I love you guys, and Michael, I missed you," she said. Michael tells Nathan, "you're my brother now, I mean that, and we got to keep each other safe for Aleahcym's sake and ours, because I guess now if I let anything happen to you, Marla will kill me," Michael said. "OK, OK, it is settled. I guess someone needs to say it. I strongly think we should name her Aleahcym," Nathan said. Then he turned toward Marla and asked, " if that is OK with you, dear?" Marla laughs," Aleahcym, It is, " she said.

"Now, you guys need to know that we are all leaving New York. Nate, you need to make some arrangements," Michael said ." Arrangements hell, I'm going with Marla!"

Nathan said in a loud voice. "Calm down, Nate. You need to let your parents know you're leaving town," explained Michael. " My parents? Since I was sixteen, I've been on my own, and it will be awesome to have a family again. Where are we going?" asked Nathan. "Dad's brother Jacob has a cabin in Hillsville, Virginia. I gave his son Ethan a call. He said it's ours as long as we need it, and it's just off the Blue Ridge Parkway, sitting on thirty-five and a half acres of land. It has a pond, creek, a natural spring, and a cave with plenty of room to raise a child." Michael said. "that sounds great. Let's pack."Marla replied. "Oh, before I forget, I got something for your two." Michael went over to his suitcase, opened it up, and pulled out the branding iron that the tribe sent to Marla. He tossed it over to Nathan, saying, "here Marla is going to need this and remember it has to be done." "And it will be," said Marla.

For the next three months, Michael struggled with being sick and feeling drained during the daylight hours but feeling fine at night. Michael awakes, not feeling very well again. It seemed Aaluk was right when the sun went down, Michael felt fine, but he stayed sick during the day and had less control of his shadow-shifting abilities. So it has been going on since he returned home. When moving day finally arrived, Michael had the moving van rented and sitting out front. After packing for three months, everyone is ready to go. Marla and Nathan start loading the van up, and Michael helps with all the big things. After the van is loaded, they just wait out the rest of the day, so when the sun sets, Michael will feel better, and they can leave. After about nine and a half hours of driving, including traffic and stops, they turn onto a gravel road. Then there it was a very long narrow gravel driveway. It has a little bridge that crosses over the little creek running across the property. They were all expecting to see a little cabin, but what there found was a nice, reasonably large three-bedroom cabin with two bathrooms, a full basement, and the upstairs was a giant study/ library. Marla and Nathan were tired, so they didn't bother unpacking the van. They found a bed and crashed, and Aaluk wasn't far behind them. Michael, on the other hand, never felt so good. At this moment, he realized that this was the best he had felt since his return home. Michael turns into the shadow wolf and takes off into the night, exploring his new surroundings.

Early the following day, the sun rose across the top of the mountains. It was a beautiful sight, thought Michael, who was still in shadow form running the grounds. Unfortunately, Michael got caught in direct sunlight as the sun topped the mountain. After that, Michael completely vanished without a trace. While back at the cabin, everyone is waking up. Nathan is in the kitchen cooking breakfast for Marla and Aaluk. Marla walks up to Nathan, kisses him, and says, "good morning." " Good morning; I can't believe this place came fully stocked with food. There was even fresh milk and eggs," said Nathan. "My uncle must have stocked it up for us," Marla responded. Aaluk set the table for them, and Nathan served up scrambled eggs, bacon, biscuits, and gravy. " Oh my goodness, Where did you learn to cook like this?" Asked Aaluk. Nathan smiled and said," once I was on my own, I had to eat, and a man can't live on popcorn alone."

"Where's Michael?" asked Marla. " I haven't seen him this morning," Nathan said. They didn't think much more about it and went about their day, unpacking the van and putting away their things. Marla, Nathan, and Aaluk sat down on the sofa to take a break when Nathan looked over at Marla and said," Marla, I know it has only been a short few months, but will you marry me."I know you are not that familiar with the ways of my tribe, but that night I marked you as my mate. We were, what would be considered married, but if you want would like a more traditional wedding ceremony, then yes, I will." Marla said. " If you say we are already married, then I'm good, but I would like to get us some bands to wear," Nathan said. It was getting late evening, and Nathan decided to start cooking dinner. "Hey, don't cook me anything. I am going hunting later; got to keep my senses up," Marla told Nathan.

"Well, Aaluk, it looks like it's just us. What do you want for dinner?"Nathan asked. "Pancakes!" she said. "OK, pancakes it is." Nathan said." Nathan, will you make Marla a plate and put it up, please," asked Aaluk. Marla opens the front door and takes a look around. She turns wolf and leaps off the porch, darting into the woods. Marla immediately picks up the scent of deer and begins tracking, which is reasonably easy considering Marla has thermal vision in werewolf form. There it was. The deer didn't have a clue Marla was around. Marla crept close and then ran and pounced her prey, tackling it to the ground as the deer was grunting and screaming for its life. Then she wraps her arms around the dears head and stops. Marla releases the deer, and it wastes no time leaving. "Marla," she heard a voice in a low whisper." Michael," Marla responds with a deep growl. She changes back into human form.

"Michael, where are you?" she asked. "I'm here," he said. "Where, Michael?" Marla asked. "Do you see the soda can? I'm in the can. Just take me home, please," Michael said. Marla picks up the can and walks home. While walking home, Michael explains to Marla, How he was in shadow form when the sun came up, and instantly he went weak. This time Michael was unable to shift back to human. The only place to hide from the sun was the soda can, where he remained all day. When they got to the cabin, Marla had the idea to completely blackout Michael's room, and she enlisted help from Nathan and Aaluk. They ducked, taped the windows, and hung blankets over them to block out all the light. Then Marla took the soda can and placed it in the room with all the lights out. Michael was able to exit the can into the room but was still unable to shift back to human. It appears he is stuck as a shadow wolf.

Later that night, Aaluk went to lay down in Michael's room to keep her brother company while Marla and Nathan went to fix the basement up for Michael. This basement had no windows, to their surprise, so they taped up around the door that exited outside. Then cut off every light in the house, and Michael went downstairs, where he could have run of the entire basement. Once Michael was settled in, everyone decided to call it a night. Marla and Nathan went to their room, and Aaluk went to hers. While in shadow form, Michael doesn't need to eat or sleep. He paces the floors and thinks about why he cannot turn human again. Finally, it hits him like a ton of bricks. The night of the attack, there was an eclipse. He yells for Marla to come quick. Marla jumps out of bed and runs down the basement stairs as fast as she can," What's wrong," she asked in a booming tone with panic in her voice?

"I need to know when the last eclipse was," Michael said. Confused, she answered, "what"? "The last eclipse, please just find out," Said Michael. "OK," Marla said. So Marla went back upstairs, grabbed her smartphone, and did an internet search. She discovered that it was early this morning, but it wasn't visible in this part of the world. So she went back downstairs and told Michael. Michael had made the connection. His shifting abilities follow eclipses. Aaluk came down the stairs and asked, "what's wrong?" "Well, I think I just figured out how the eclipse affects my shifting abilities, Michael said. " I forgot to tell you that Grandma told me, to tell you, that at the peak of any eclipse, solar or lunar, you could get stuck, temporally in whatever form you are in at the peak of the eclipse," said Aaluk. "Well, thank you, Aaluk. This morning would have been better timing," said Michael. "Oops, I'm off to bed goodnight," Aaluk said.

Chapter Seven

The Great Betrayal

The following day Nathan got up early, just before the sun rose, kissed Marla, and told her he was going for a run before breakfast. Nathan decides to stray from his standard path and bolts off. Nathan heard what sounded like a truck door slam and went to investigate. While he is running in the sound he heard, he can see a brown truck with blue emergency lights through the trees. It appears to be the game warden. From out of nowhere, a great big brown bear stands up on the right side of Nathan, and volatility smacks him down to the ground and claws and mauls him. After the bear is convinced that Nathan is no longer a threat, it leaves.

Back at the cabin, everyone is getting up. Marla and Aaluk are making breakfast Michael is still stuck in his room.

When a truck pulls up the driveway, A tall, slender lady with long red hair jumps out of the truck, covered in blood, screaming for help—Marla dashes out the door. " I've already radioed for rescue. They will have to land a chopper in your field," she said. Marla looked in the back of the truck," Oh my gosh, Nathan," she said. "What the hell happened." "it looks like he got too close to a brown bear. Help me stop the bleeding!" she said.

The helicopter arrived, and they loaded Nathan up, and he was off to the hospital. " My name is Aby. I appreciate your help," she said. " I got to find out where that helicopter is going; that's my husband. "said Marla. " follow me, and I'll show you how to get there," Aby said. Marla and Aaluk all loaded up in the truck and followed Aby to the hospital, about a two-hour drive. It was a long, quiet drive. Marla sobbed the whole way, expecting the worse. Aaluk just sat there quietly. Once at the hospital, they learn that Nathan is in I.C.U critical condition and in a coma. The Doctor is not sure when or even if he will recover. Aby leaves because she has to return the county vehicle. Marla and Aaluk stay there with Nathan. Later that night, Aby returns, and to everyone's surprise, she brings them dinner. She is very concerned for Nathan. Aby and Marla seem to be hitting it off rather well. Marla could use a friend right now.

Months and months have gone by, and Aby has gone with Marla almost every other day after work to visit with Nathan. Marla and Aby have gotten to be close friends. After about three months, Nathan's wounds have mostly healed, but he remains in a coma, and because his wounds are not life-threatening anymore, he will need to be moved to a nursing home for coma patients. Marla, who is now almost seven months pregnant, makes the long trip with Aby and Aaluk every weekend to see Nathan. They were late getting back from the nursing home one Saturday night, so Marla invited Aby to crash at the cabin. Aby accepted the invitation because she was exhausted and didn't feel like she could drive anymore. "Aaluk, wakey wakey eggs, and bakey guess what? We are going to have a slumber party," Aby said. Aaluk stretches out her arms to Aby."Auntie Aby, will you sleep in my room with me?" Aaluk asks.

"You know I will," Aby said. "you make a great auntie," Marla tells Aby. "Thank you," Aby said. Everyone manages to make it into the house. Marla shows Aby around the house, and when she gets to the basement door, she stops. "These stairs go into the basement, my brother Michael has claimed the entire basement, and he is a night owl," Marla said. Then she takes Aby to Aaluk's room," alright, you two don't slumber party too hard."Marla told them. They laughed and went on to bed. Marla walked back to the basement, opened the door, and walked down the stairs." Michael, we're back," she said. "I know. It sounds like you brought company. You two have gotten to be pretty close; it is about time you made a friend. How's

Nate? Said Michael. Marla takes a deep breath and sighs,"

the same," she said. "He will get better," Michael tells her.

" I know. I love you, bro," she said. Marla heads back

upstairs, but she decides to go outside instead of the bed.

She is just standing there on the porch thinking when she

hears some branches breaking in the woods. Marla thinks to

herself, what if it is that bear. Then like a flash of lighting,

she starts running in the direction of the sound, and in mid-

stride, she turns wolf and begins to track down her victim.

She is hot on its trail. Marla slows down, and she goes into

stalking mode, she can see it, and it is a brown bear. She

creeps closer, closer, then BAMB! She is on it, ripping

apart. It s a gruesome sight before the bear even has time to

react to Marla's attack. It was a mutilated pile of blood and

guts lying on the cold ground.

Marla turns human. She is naked, holding her

pregnant belly, while in the middle of the pile of guts,

covered in the bear's blood and entrails. She drops to he

knees and begins crying frantically, and with a clenched

fist, she looks up at the sky. A giant yellow moon is

directly behind her as she screams out Nathan's name. After

her meltdown, she pulls herself together and gradually

walks back to the creek. Then gracefully steps down into

the water and washes off the blood. Then she quietly

sneaks into the house to take a shower and goes on to bed.

Hours later, Aby wakes up, feeling the urge to use the

bathroom. She gets up and patters barefoot down the hall.

As she walks by the basement door, she can hear the

television. She proceeds to the bathroom. On her way back,

she stops at the basement door. She listens for a minute,

opens the door, and steps down onto the first step."

Michael," softly she whispers. "Marla," said Michael. "No,

it is Aby. I don't think we've met yet," she said. "Oh, don't

come down here. I'm not decent," he said. Aby sits down

on the stairs and proceeds to make small talk with Michael.

Aby loves to listen to Michael talk and seems not to mind that she can't see his face. Time seemed to fly by, and they had talked all night before either of them realized it. It was almost morning when Michael glanced over at the clock on the television stand. "Wow, Aby, It's the morning. We probably should get some rest," said Michael. "Your right. I have truly enjoyed talking to you. Maybe we can talk again soon, I hope," said Aby. "By the way, your very beautiful Aby," said Michael. Aby blushes and walks back to Aaluk's room, smiling and humming. Michael has left her feeling very warm-hearted inside, and she cannot wait to talk to him again.

The following day Marla wakes early. She starts a pot of coffee and grabs a bagel. She sits down at the kitchen table, lays her head in her hands, and takes a moment to think. After a few minutes, she could hear footsteps walking down the hallway, and in a delighted voice, Aby said, " I smell coffee." Marla smiles. "There is my best-est friend in the whole wide world. How did you sleep? " I didn't sleep much, but it was a wonderful night. I got up some time to go to the bathroom and sat on your brother's steps talking all night," Aby said. "That is awesome, but I need to warn you, my brother has, well, it's more of a, hmm, condition for lack of a better word. You can't be in the same room with my brother, I can't explain right now, you will just have to trust me," Marla said. "No problem, can I come back tonight and stay? You, me, and Aaluk can play some cards or something," Aby said, "Yes, that would be awesome." said Marla. Marla and Aby pour themselves a cup of coffee and talk for a bit longer, then Aby gets up and leaves for work. Marla makes breakfast for Aaluk and then starts her daily cleaning ritual.

Aaluk wakes up at the smell of breakfast and goes to the kitchen. Before she can even sit down, she becomes very sick and runs to the bathroom. Marla is right behind her, making sure she is OK. They suspect that she has a stomach bug. That whole day Aaluk spends in and out of the bathroom. When Aby returns that evening, she isn't feeling very well herself. She complains that it is her stomach. She explains to Marla that she will not be able to go with her to see Nathan tomorrow, but she offers to stay and watch Aaluk so Marla can see Nathan. Marla insists that she stay and take care of both of them. Aby insists that Marla should go and that everything will be fine at the house. Marla decides to listen to Aby and will go to see Nathan tomorrow. The following day Marla wakes and begins to get ready to leave. Aby gets up feeling a little better than yesterday, and Aaluk is sleeping in after being sick all night. Marla walks into Aaluk's room, leans over, and kisses her forehead," I love you, pumpkin. I hope you feel better today," Marla whispers.

Then Marla grabs her things, hugs Aby, and shouts," goodbye, Michael." She is out the door. Aby walks to Michael's room, lightly knocks on the door, and asks," are you up, Michael?" "Yes, I am. Are you feeling better today?" asked Michael. " Yeah, my stomach is a little queasy, but I am OK," she said. Aaluk walks to the basement door, " good morning Aby," Then she gives Aby a big good morning hug and says, " I'm glad you're here today." "aw, honey, I'm glad to be here," said Aby. Then Aaluk walks to the living room and turns on the television. Aby sits on the steps and sighs. "What's wrong?" Michael asked. "Nothing," said Aby. Michael and Aby do a lot of talking. They are getting to know each other. The more time Aby spends with Michael, the more she loves spending it with him.

Chapter Eight.

The Waughy Princess

Later that morning, Marla arrives at the nursing home. She sits down beside Nathan's bed and reads the children's book that he picked out for their baby. She reads," The Waughy Princess, By Sir Bach Napall, page one. Once upon a time, a beautiful Princess lived in an enchanted world. One morning Waughy woke up from a very disturbing nightmare. It was so distressing that it almost seemed very real to her. In her nightmare, a woman's voice sounded very, very, very sad. The voice was pleading with Waughy to wake up. Then she heard a man's voice, and it was telling her, "you need to journey to the sea of disbelief, and then she would believe." So said the man's voice. The sea of Disbelief isn't very far away, so she decides to go.

Waughy straps her stuffed bear, Leo, on her back and leaves the castle, and she is off to the sea. She is thinking and wondering questions about what if and why? Along the way, she meets Mr. Tippers. Mr. Tippers is a very likable troll, and he stands slightly hunched over so that he is about Waughy's size. "Hello'" he said. " Hello to you, Sir," Waughy replies. " Aw, you look sad, is everything OK?" he asked. "Not really, I had a dream that a sad lady was telling me to wake up, and then a man's voice told me to go to the Sea Of Disbelief, and then I would believe," she told him. "hmm. It seems odd to me to travel to the Sea Of Disbelief in order to believe, but can I go with you? I want to see the sea," he said.

Waughy laughs, and she agrees to let him tag along, and together they go on their way. In the distance, they can see the sea. They also noticed that the sky was very dark with a storm cloud over the sea. Lighting strikes the water, and water spouts rise out of the sea. The closer they got, the more the wind blew and the darker the sky became.

"Waughy, I'm scared," Mr. Tippers said. "Me too, but we must go on," Waughy replied. " Why must we carry on?" he said. "I'm not sure, but I know that I have to. You stay here. You should be safe here," she said. "does staying here mean being alone," said Mr. Tippers. "Yes!" Waughy exclaimed. " O..Tay what-chew,wait-in on, let's go get that sea!" Mr. Tippers said in an amusing troll voice, so they braved the storm and pressed forward. "Waughy, you need to enter the water," a voice from above said. "Wow! your so popular that even the clouds speak to you," said Mr. Tippers. "Yeah, that's crazy. I must be napping. Quick wake me up," Waughy said. "One problem with that theory, I'm not asleep!" he shouted with panic in his voice. " You're right. You stay here, Mr. Tippers. I'm going in," she said. She begins walking into the water, Thunder booming, lightning striking around her. Mr. Tippers yells," Waughy no you, can..., bark, wolf," suddenly, Mr. Tippers is barking, growling like a dog. Then a colossal water spout swallows Waughy up, and then it was over. Waughy is now staring into an empty void of blackness. She can hear a dog faintly barking as if it were very distant. Then a man's voice," look, she's trying to open her eyes," the voice said. " Oh my goodness, Kimmy, Kimmy, Oh, come on baby, can you hear me waughy," said a woman's voice. Waughy's eyes open "Mom, Dad, what's going on? Where am I?" "You were in an accident, baby. You're in the hospital. You've been asleep for three months. Oh, my sweet baby, you're awake now!" She said, crying. The dog barks, "Mr. Tipper's there you are." Waughy said. A nurse has been standing at the door, and she asks," If you don't mind me asking? How did you guy's come up with Waughy as a nickname?" Waughy's mom responds," When she learned how to talk, she could not say I love you. She said I waughy." After a few tests, Kimmy was released from the hospital, and the family lived happily ever after. The end.

With tear-filled eyes, Marla reaches over and places her hand on Nathan's forehead. She said, "please wake up, baby. I miss you so badly. Our baby is almost here. She is kicking more and more every day. She is due any day now; please come home." There is nothing, no response, no extra monitor activity, nothing. Nathan's lifeless body lies there. Marla sobs. She leaves and starts the long drive home.

Chapter Nine

A Kiss To Remember

While back at the cabin, Aby is cooking dinner, and Aaluk is in Michael's room. Once dinner is ready, Aby set's the table and call's for Aaluk and gets no response. She was worried, so she looked for her and couldn't find her. She finds Aaluk in the basement laughing like she and Michael are playing together. Aby can't take it anymore; she has to get into Michael's room. Aby creeps to the door to his room and can hear them clowning around and laughing. She bursts into Michael's room and sees Aaluk on the bed, with a small night light turned on above her head. When they see Aby, Michael, and Aaluk both shout as if in one voice, "Don't turn on the lights!" Aby is confused but doesn't turn the lights on. " OK, sounds like you guys are having a party in here, and I didn't get invited; and Michael, why are you hiding from me" she replies, " I'm not hiding from you," he replies. Aby sits down on the bed beside Aaluk, lays her head in her hands, and cries. "Don't cry, auntie Aby," Aaluk said with a sorrowful voice, and then she told him, "Michael, please just show her." Michael shadow shifts into an image of himself as a person, and on the wall, you can see him walking over to the wall directly in front of Aby. With her head still buried deep inside her hands, sobbing, Aby lets out a long sigh. She says," Michael, I know you're a shadow shifter, I know Marla is a werewolf, and I know Aleahcym is going to someone exceptional. I know Aaluk talks to her deceased family members, and she talks in her sleep a lot; that's how I know these things." still crying, she continues by saying, "and I just wanted you guys to trust me, you guys make me believe I'm family, but yet you don't let me be apart of the family." Micheal is stunned, but quickly recovers and says" lookup." Aby look's up at the shadow of the man in front of her. Then Michael tells her," I'm sorry I made you feel that way. I want you to know all things we've talked about and getting to know each other and the feeling we shared that is real, and that is still me. I didn't think you would understand, and I'm sorry." Aaluk Hugs Aby, and she says, "OK, now let's play shadow charades" they all start laughing.

So Aby, Michael, and Aaluk are all in Michael's room. They are playing Aaluk's favorite game, shadow charades, and Aby is playing along also. Michael's shadow shifts into different animal forms, and they try to guess the animal's name. "OK, little girl, it is time for bed," Aby said. Yawning, " I know, I'm going goodnight. I love you, Michael, and auntie Aby," said Aaluk. " I love you," they replied at the same time. Jinx, you owe me a kiss," Aby said. "A kiss. I thought it was a Coke," said Michael.

" Well, we're playing the adult version," she said. Michael's shadow moves to the wall next to Aby's shadow, and then he responds. " I wish I could kiss you, Aby, but unfortunately for me right now, unless you're a shadow shifter, I'm just a dark figure on the wall," Michael said desperately. Aby stands up and positions herself to cast her shadow in front of Michael's on the wall. She moves her arms to look like they are around his hips and leans her body in so that the shadow of her face is at just the right angle. Then her lips pop together, making a kissing sound. " I love you, Michael," she said. " I love you too," Michael replies. " I will be back," I will tuck in Aaluk," she said. Aby leaves Michael's room and walks into Aaluk's room. Aby kisses her forehead and tells her that she loves her and goodnight. Then she walks back to Michael's room and turns off the night light they were using to cast shadows on the wall. she strips off all her clothes and climbs into Michael's bed. "Goodnight, Michael, Maybe this could be

used as an incentive to find a way to become human again,"
Aby said. Michael, not focused on the topic, responds," uh
goodnight, you know I don't sleep right," Michael said. "
I'm counting on it and hoping you will find a way to keep
me from sleeping," she said. Then she pulled the thin,
sheet-like cover over her and rolled over to her side. "
goodnight," she said. Michael fake cries, " maybe for you,
but even shadows have hard feelings. I'm glad the lights are
off," Michael said with a laugh. " You know it has occurred
to me that you don't know what I look like; you might not
find me attractive once I'm human," Michael said. " You do
know your sisters have pictures, and I have seen them all,"
she said. " not the one at that," Aby interrupts "party? seen
it," She said. "Aw, man," Michael sighs. " Go to sleep, "
Michael tells her in a joking manner. Aby chuckles and
tries to go to sleep.

Late that night, Marla returns home. She goes to Aaluk's
room, sneaking in. She kisses Aaluk and then exits. Her

next stop is Michael's room; she opens the basement door, then walks down the stairs. She turns on the light, and to her surprise, Aby jumps up out of bed, "Marla, your home!" she says, " Wow, you're in Michael's bed and naked. How is that working out?" Marla said with excitement in her voice. " Not like I wanted it to," Aby replied. " Hey, you guys mind killing that light," said Michael. "Michael, where are you at?" asks Marla. "under the bed, you know I can't see in the light, and that it makes me weak and sick," Michael said. Marla turns off the light. "Sorry, Michael, I guess I don't have to keep covering up my brother's secret, and from the looks of things, you seem to be OK with it?" Marla said." Or yours, I know you're a wolf. I've seen you change. I didn't say anything because I was afraid I would lose you as my friend, and I don't want that; you're like a sister to me. My job wanted me to find out what was killing the deer in the area, and once I figured out that it was you killing the deer. I told my job it was a large population of bobcats and coyotes. They wanted me to set up game cameras, and when I argued that this land was private property, they fired me. I have found four cameras since then on your ground and destroyed them. Please don't make me leave. I have no place else to go."Aby said.

`"No one is going to make you leave. Our home is your home, as long as you want it to be." Marla said. Then Marla and Michael explain their family's history to Aby. Michael tells Aby to reach under his bed and take out the box. Aby did. When she opened it, she found the branding iron. Michael explains to Aby how they need her help because Marla isn't going to be able to brand Aleahcym, and I can't seem to hold material objects at the moment. Aby panics, shaking her head no while saying," I don't think I can do that to a tiny baby." Marla pulls back her hair, revealing the mark behind her ear. she says, "Aaluk is marked; this has become the mark of our tribe." After a bit,

Aby calms down, and she agrees to do it.

Chapter Ten

The Birth

The following day, Aby get 's up and walks into the hallway, Where to her surprise, she finds Marla on the floor curled into a ball, crying. "Oh my gosh, Marla, are you OK?" Aby said. "It's happening, The baby is coming, but something isn't right. It feels like she is clawing her way out." Marla said. " How is that possible?" asked Aby. Aaluk runs through the house, turns off the lights, and closes all the blinds so that Michael can come into the hallway, "your need to turn," Michael said. Marla makes the change, and after a short labor, Marla gives birth to her baby. For the first time, a child has been born as a wolf.

Because the baby is in wolf form, Marla has to be in wolf form to deliver. If not, Marla would've died during the birth. Aby heats the stove eye and places the branding iron on it until the iron glows a bright cherry red. Aby takes the hot iron into the hallway, Aaluk raises the newborn's left ear, and Aby gently places the branding iron on her. Then both baby and Marla begin to scream and howl like banshees. Afterward, baby Aleahcym changes into human form, and so does Marla simultaneously. Marla takes her baby, and they go off to rest and let nature heal them both. Aby and Aaluk clean up the mess.

Months later, Marla and Aleahcym are doing very well. Marla has Aleahcym's ears pierced and silver studs put in them to prevent her from making the change while she is still a baby. However, when Aleahcym hits her teens, Marla knows that her body will know what to do, and Aleahcym will be able to change at will after some practice. Marla has also found out that she has a unique link to her child. Everything her baby feels or experiences, Marla can feel.

Aaluk loves her new role as auntie Aaluk, and she plays the part very well. Aby and Michael have been inseparable.

Almost a year has passed now. One morning Aby gets up and calls for Michael. "Michael, baby, I got a surprise for you, but I'm not sure if it will work, so you will have to humor me." "OK, what's up?" Michael asked. Aby walks over to her dresser, and in her top drawer, she pulls out a jewelry box. She opened the box and inside laid a necklace. It was a small hollowed-out heart that was fashioned out of black onyx, and the tip of the arrow going through it had a small diamond laid in it. The top of the arrow was a pearl ball that pulled out like a cork in a bottle, and in gold letters across the heart was the name Aleahcym.

" I had this made for you," Aby said. "That's nice, but you spelled my name wrong," Michael said, joking. "Silly boy, it will go to Aleahcym when she is older," Aby said. Aby uncorks the heart and closes the door to the room, so there is no light. "I want you to try to get into this heart," Aby said. Michael agreed and was able to move into the heart without any trouble. Aby corks the heart, puts the necklace around her neck, and then turns on the lights. "Michael, can you hear me?" Aby said. "Yes, I can, can you hear me?" she said. "Yes," Michael replied. "Now the fun part, but only if you are up for it," Aby tells Michael, "what?" he said. "We are going to go for a walk outside in the sunshine. If this doesn't work, scream, and I'll run back to your room and let you out."Aby said to him. "I haven't been outside in forever. Let's try it," said Michael. Aby starts walking throughout the house, standing in front of the windows, and all is going well. She walked to the front door and opened it slowly," you ready?" she said. "Let's do this!" yelled Michael from inside the heart. She steps out the door, onto the porch, and then walks out into the yard, facing the heart and Michael in full direct sunlight. Michael starts shouting, "YES, YOU'RE A GENIUS, THIS IS

AWESOME!" " I take it that it's working," Aby said. "If I didn't feel like a genie trapped in a lamp, I'd kiss you right now," Michael said. Aby takes Michael back inside, and then she takes off the necklace and places it around Aleahcym's neck. " Now, you too can help babysit," she said with laughter. "I'd loved to," he said. " If only Asterisk could see me now," Aby mummers under her breath. "What, what did you say," said Marla. "Nothing. Why?" Aby said. Then at that exact moment in time, Aby secretly slides a knife into her hand and lunges forward, thrusting the blade through Aaluk's heart. Michael desperately tries to escape the necklace but cannot do anything but watch in horror.

"This child is to be delivered to Asterisk. Michael, I hope you enjoy that prison," Aby shouts. Then she shapeshifts into a brown bear and turns her attack toward Marla. Marla goes werewolf, and the fight is on. Marla and Aby go at it for hours. The house is in shambles, and broken glass is everywhere. Finally, Aby climbs on top of the countertops and jumps at Marla. Marla grabs the broom and holds it at an angle. Aby collides with Marla, and blood is everywhere. Marla's throat has been slashed wide open, and Aby has been impaled through the heart with the broom. Marla turns into a human and crawls her way to the cell phone lying on the floor. She reaches it and dials 911, and then she collapses dead on the floor. The police arrive to what looks like a scene straight from a horror movie. They try to determine just what the hell happened. They didn't have a clue, with all the claw marks, bear and wolf tracks, and three bodies. Aleahcym was taken into police custody until they could contact her next of kin.

The police track Jacob down and notify him of the vicious animal attack on his nieces. He decides to take in Aleahcym and raise her as his own. He is sorry for what has happened but doesn't mourn for Marla and Aaluk since he had only met Marla and Michael once or twice when they were children and has never even met Aaluk. He and the police tried their best to locate Michael, but it was as if he had dropped off the earth's face.

Aleahcym has always known throughout her young years that somehow she was different from all the other children. When Ethan would bring his family over, she felt like she didn't fit in. She always preferred to play alone, or go to her hide-out spot, a small cave deep inside the forest but still within earshot, for her anyway. Aleahcym has always felt that she is at one with the forest, and with good reason. Even with the silver earrings in her ears, she begins changing into her wolf form at eight years old. She has learned a lot about herself, like she has her timid form, which she transforms into most of the time, where she turns into a beautiful white-furred snow wolf, with a gray diamond-like patch on the top of her head, in between her ears. She has big bright sapphire blue eyes, with a brown star bust around her pupils. What makes her unique is her other form, which isn't so beautiful; she becomes the beast when she is upset or angered. The beast is a big, ugly, bi-pedal werewolf capable of ripping your head off with a single swipe of her incredibly long, sharp claws. Even in this form, she is in complete control of her actions. Which means she's smart and deadly. She learns and suspects that Jacob isn't her real dad as time goes by. But she never questions him about it. She figures that one day when he is ready, he will tell her all about it, between school and her best friends, Tiara and Hope, and don't forget boys, that doesn't leave a lot of time to worry about it.

Fall is creeping up on her little town. She is excited; fall and winter are her favorite seasons. There is something about the cool air and the falling leaves and when the snowfalls. Aleahcym knows that she is perfectly camouflaged with her surroundings. Being concealed is very important to her because this is the time of the year. She likes to play her favorite game, hunt the hunter.

Although Jacob's land is posted, a few hunters apparently cannot read the signs, so she finds it fun to change into her timid form and scare them off the property. She has been doing this for a few years, and she is good at it. One brisk November morning, Aleahcym wakes to her alarm clock blaring" BEEP BEEP," she reaches up, turns it off, climbs out of bed, and starts to get ready for school. She glances out her window and catches sight of two blaze orange vests, making their way across the fence line and disappearing. After finishing up her morning routine, she has a brief conversation with her dad (Jacob) and finds out that he hasn't given anyone permission to hunt on their land. She is out the door and off to school.

Once at school, it's the same ole grind, students talking in the halls, jocks playing basketball in the gym before class, and everyone else is waiting in the cafeteria for the bell to chime, to signal it's time for class. While in the cafeteria, Chad approaches her. You know the type. They think they have a free pass to do whatever they want. But, they also have a what the hell are you going to do about it attitude. yeah, that type." Blondie, I did your daddy a favor this morning; you don't think he'll miss those no trespassing signs do you," he said with a mocking character. "Not as much as you will," she said. "Come on, that's it, that's all the come back you got?" he asks. She ignores him and walks away. She feels a peck on her shoulder; it's Caiden, Chad's slightly younger brother," Hey, I'm sorry about my brother, and I didn't know it was your land we were on; I'll put the signs back up," he told her. "No, it's OK, we're cool, but please don't hunt on our land," she said." I won't," he said.

The following weekend, early on Saturday morning, Aleahcym gets up. Being very sneaky, she opens her bedroom window, climbs out onto the roof, leaps to the tree limb hanging over the rooftop, and then climbs down to the porch below her. Her favorite song enters her head. Once her feet hit the ground, she changes into her timid wolf form, and dart's off into the forest, signing. She lifts her nose to the air and picks up Chad's scent, and the song in her head quickly changes to another fast-paced song, she lets out a long, wicked-sounding howl, and like lighting streaking across a stormy sky, she races to his position in the forest. Her heart is pounding with every stride, anticipating Chad's reactions and thinking of her every counteraction or attack. Finally, she sees Chad stealthily creeping up behind him. Chad hears the leaves slightly crunch behind him and quickly turns. Aleahcym snarls and gives a vicious low growl. Chad slings the rifle over from his shoulder, laying a bead down between her eyes, his finger pressed tightly on the trigger. He begins breathing through his nose and releasing his breath slowly out of his mouth as he squeezes the trigger. Then as if from out of thin air, appeared Caiden. He tackles Chad to the ground, "BOOM," a shot fires off, hitting the tree beside Aleahcym.

Chad pins Caiden to the ground and draws his fist back to punch him. Aleahcym pounces Chad and rolls him off Caiden, putting herself in between them with Caiden to her backside, growling and snarling and showing her teeth at Chad. Chad trembles in fear.

Aleahcym crouches down low, lets out a vicious bark, leaps clear over Chad, and runs off into the woods. At that moment, Chad wet his pants. "Just what in the hell are you doing, Caiden? You better not tell a soul about this." "About which part, the big bad wolf, or you pissing yourself," said Caiden, laughing, then covering it up with a fake cough. "I think I understand why they don't want us hunting here," said Chad. "Look, man, you're my brother, and I don't want to see you get in trouble. Plus, I like her and don't need you messing it up for me," Caiden said. The boys are walking and cutting up with each other, and they come up on Aleahcym's hideout. They could see Aleahcym pulling her tight skinny jeans back up around her slender body from a distance. " Everything OK?" asked Caiden. "Yep, I was catching up on some reading when I heard you two messing around," she said. "Do you always read naked, in the middle of the woods? Oh, let me guess, a romance novel," said Chad smiling from ear to ear. " Sorry, little boy, I had to step around the cave to pee, and I at least like to take my pants off first," she gives a slight grunt, like she's clearing her throat, and then says," maybe you should try it," pointing down at his pants. Embarrassed, he drops his head, turns around, and walks away. "Hey, I'm sorry, Chad, don't walk away. I won't tell anyone. I want us all to be friends, not to hate each other; come on, man, what do you say?" she said. Chad turns toward them, walks up to Aleahcym, reaches out his hand, and says," Hi, I'm Chad, you may not know this about me, but I'm not such a bad guy," he said. "Hi, Chad, nice to finally meet you.

You guys can hunt here if you want, but not on this side of the property near the cave, and no shooting toward my house," she tells them. "After my experience today, I'll never hunt this land. You and your dad need to be careful around here," Chad said. "Why, what happened?" she asked, pretending she didn't already know. Chad and Caiden tell her about the wolf they encountered and explain the experience to her, " Do you come out here a lot?" Chad asked. "Yes," said Aleahcym. "You might want to keep a cell phone handy," he said. "Wow, Chad, you act as if you care," she said. "I do care, Caiden is crushing on you, and I can't have you get eaten by a wolf. Before he can ask you out, there would be no living with him," Chad told her. In a very harsh, disgruntled voice," Thanks, bro," said Caiden. "OK, my work here is done. I'll see you at the house, little brother," said Chad. He picks up his rifle and walks off. " You be careful out here," Caiden tells her. Aleahcym shy's away and then tells him. "I will, but it won't do me any good to carry my cell phone if I don't have your number," Caiden and Aleahcym exchange numbers and talk for just a few minutes. In reality, they've been talking for hours.

They reluctantly part ways. It is getting dark, so Caiden

walks Aleahcym home. They were both getting a little

freaked out through the darkened forest. At one point,

Caiden thought he saw a person's silhouette in the distance.

As they got closer, it was gone. He dismissed it as his eyes

playing tricks on him. "do you see that?" Aleahcym asked.

"Who is that?" asked Caiden. " Hello, is someone there? I'll

bet your brother is trying to be funny," she tells him. " I

don't think that's Chad," he replies, sounding a little

creeped out. Then the figure dissipates into thin air, right

before both their eyes. " You believe in ghosts," asked

Caiden. " I do now," said Aleahcym. Once they arrive at

Aleahcym's house, they talk for a few minutes, Caiden tells

her goodnight, but they agree to talk on the cell phones

until he makes it back home. Aleahcym dials his number,

sits down on the porch steps, and they talk while he walks

the long two miles home. Once he makes it home, they say their goodbyes, and she enters her house.

"You're getting in a little late. Everything alright?" Jacob asked. "Everything is more than alright; everything is perfect," she said. "OK, who's the boy," he said. "Oh, dad," she said, smiling. " Anyway, I would like to discuss something with you," he tells her. "What, dad?" she curiously asked. Jacob reaches into his pocket and takes out the necklace he had put up in the cabinet when she was a baby. " This is yours, this is going to be a lot to think about, but I want you to know the truth," Before he could even finish his sentence, she interrupts," Look, I figured out your not my real dad long ago. Still, you are my dad in my heart and always have been. I love you, daddy," Their eyes welled up with tears while she was talking. She wraps her arms tightly around his neck. " He raises her hair slightly off her neck and clasps the necklace together. "You were wearing this the night I got you," he said. Then he sits her down and explains to her the terrifying story and how and why he got the great honor of raising and calling her his own. She took it well, but she was upset to know the facts.

After some time passes, she tends not to dwell on it so much, and she seems more content focusing her time on Caiden. They have become close, and she has already met his parents, and tonight he gets to meet her dad. Jacob has dinner ready at 6:00 pm sharp. Looking out her bedroom window, she can see Caiden driving up the long gravel driveway in his daddy's truck. She nervously runs downstairs "he's here!" she shouts. " Calm down, baby. It's just a boy," he says, grinning from ear to ear.

Caiden knocks on the door, and Aleahcym takes off to the door to greet him. Jacob welcomes him into their home, and they all sit down to dinner. After dinner and a couple of hours of talking, Aleahcym and Caiden invite Jacob to go for a walk with them, he declines, and they go on without him, as they both hoped he wouldn't accept their invitation. They walk around the property line, and Caiden asks Aleahcym if they can go steady. She accepts. He takes her hand in his as they walk around. "You know what, let's make it official that we are together," she said. Then she takes off her necklace and leans in close to him, placing the chain around his neck, their lips almost touching, and just before they could kiss, he turns into a shadow, and Aleahcym falls through him onto the ground.

Very confused," What the hell," she said. Caiden freaked out" I'm a ghost," he said. They both sit down on the ground to figure out what is happening. A voice from out of nowhere" dude, calm down; it's OK. Focus your thoughts on being solid again, and you will be," the voice told him Caiden took a deep breath, calmed down, collected his thoughts, and instantly he was his old no shadow self again. "Thanks, man, Caiden said, " Who are you talking to?"

asked Aleahcym. "The guy that told me how to become human again," he said. " I need to know whether you got weak or sick while you were a shadow," said the voice. " No," Caiden said. "Grab the pearl ball of the top of the necklace and pull it like your unplugging a cork," said the voice from the necklace. Caiden grabs the pearl part of the necklace and pulls; the necklace makes a "pop" and like thick black smoke billowing out the top of a volcano, out of the necklace came Michael. In the form of a shadow werewolf, he tries to change into his human form but is still unable. Before Michael can speak or explain, Aleahcym, feeling very threatened, turns into her big, bad, super wolf form and stands to confront Michael, ready to fight. "Aleahcym, is it you?" asked Michael. "Who wants to know," she said. "I'm your uncle, your mom's brother," he said. Feeling less threatened, she changes human again. After everyone takes a deep breath, the tension settles a bit. Michael explained to Aleahcym everything and left nothing out. Caiden listens and takes it all in as Michael explains why they need to be preparing for war because it is coming. Then Michael explains how he cannot be in the daylight; he glances over at Caiden and says," This is not your fight; you can leave," Caiden determined that he isn't going anywhere. "OK, my girlfriend is a werewolf, and her uncle, a shadow wolf, whom I might add, turned me into a ghost today, and now you want me to leave? No way! I got an idea I wear you in the necklace during the daylight hours, and if something were to happen, I could go ghost and possibly help, and in the evenings, I'll let you out. I leave the bottle open for you; when you return, wake me I'll cork you up before daylight," Caiden said. "OK, we need to train in daylight and darkness; Caiden find a sword; I have an idea; we will meet first thing in the morning," Michael said. They walked Aleahcym back home; Michael returned to the necklace when they got to the house. Caiden turns to Aleahcym," I guess this is goodnight," he said. They finally share their first kiss. Caiden walks to his truck in a joyful daze and drives home. Aleahcym is full of smiles; she walks to her room and gets ready for bed.

The very next morning, Caiden climbs out of bed. He dresses in his desert-style camouflaged fatigues. And a long black hooded trench coat to finish off his new look. He adds a skull face bandanna mask and then grabs the dragon sword hanging on his wall for decoration. "Dude is this Halloween?" asked Michael. "No, but if you're going to train me to be a badass, we might as well look like one," said Caiden. Michael replies," I like your style, kid; let's do this." Caiden walks to the full-length mirror hanging on his closet door, "let's see how we look," he says to Michael. he looks in the mirror, grabs the outside edge of the cloak, and thrusts it around his body, while at the same time concentrating on becoming a shadow. Just as the mantle blanketed him completely, he becomes a black transparent shadow, sporting his new fashion attire, sword included.

Then he walks up to his bedroom door and says to Michael, " You know I have to try it, right?" Before Michael could say anything, Caiden walks fast toward the door and passes straight through it. Chad's bedroom opens, and Caiden immediately turns back to himself without even thinking about it. "Who are you talking to?" said Chad. "Myself, bro, go back to bed, man," Caiden told him. Then makes his way down the hall and out to the truck.

Once in the truck, Michael says to Caiden," wow, you seem to be a natural at this; how did you know you could pass through the door," "I didn't," Caiden replied. Then they both start laughing. And after a short drive. They arrive at Aleahcym's house. She meets them outside, "I have to tell you something." Aleahcym said." I know why you can share Michael's shadow-shifting ability. A woman appeared to me last night, almost like a dream. But I wasn't sleeping, her name was Asaaluk, and she shared with me my family history and how all living beings have a life force.

Everyone's life force vibrates at different frequencies, but you and Michael share the same frequency. That is why you can shadow shift while you're wearing the necklace, and she said it's the reason you met, and we have to go wake my dad, my real dad Nathan," she told them. "OK then, I guess we are off to Roanoke. Did she happen to say how to wake him," asked Michael? " She said the only way to wake him out of the coma is for me to turn him. And it's not going to be an easy task. Because he will be a werewolf when he wakes, doing this quiet will be a challenge. We may have to stay as much as a week, waiting on his transition. And baby, I love the look. If you weren't sharing my uncle's soul right now, I'd so kiss you," she said. Caiden shrugs his shoulders, lowers his head, and says," It wasn't my fault." "We train first to learn to work as a team, and then we wake Nathan because we could use another wolf on our team. You have no idea what we are going to be up against," Michael said

Michael explains how they will be up against shape and shadow shifters, how both can be wounded and, or killed in their human form but very hard to kill in their shifted forms, and how that shadow shifters can bring harm to you in either state, but can only be harmed by another shadow shifter.

While the group trains, they're blissfully unaware that Enoch has massed together a small army of shape and shadow shifters. And have been on a global mission to genocide werewolves off the face of the earth. Enoch was raised to believe that werewolves are evil and out to erase all shifters from existence. Although he is up in his years, he has raised his army under these same beliefs. The only way to become a shape or shadow shifter is genetic, except for Aleahcym and Michael's sporadic case. The werewolf virus is stored in their saliva, so if bitten by one, if you don't seek antibiotics to kill the bacterial infection, then the werewolf virus will run its course through your body, and then transformation begins.

Chapter Eleven

The Dragon and the Void

After training for weeks, The group is confident they can work together. Their first task is close at hand, waking Nathan. They plan to go in a few weeks while school is out for Christmas break. The three of them are out at the cafe, talking amongst themselves, trying to formulate a plan. Still, they can't figure out how to sneak a new turned raging werewolf out of quiet old folks' home without drawing any attention to themselves or causing someone to have a heart attack in the process. After practice, they head home. Aleahcym explains to Jacob that she found her dad and that she and Caiden were going to the nursing home to stay with him over Christmas vacation. Jacob gives his permission, and their plan is ready to begin.

The day has finally arrived. They load up in the pick-up, throw their belongings in the back, and go to the nursing home. After a two-hour drive, they pull into the parking lot. They walk up to Nathans's room. Aleahcym feels excited, nervous, and sad all at the same time. Aleahcym walks up to her dad. She weeps after looking at his face for the first time in her life. They all bide their time until they feel like the moment is right. Aleahcym steps into the private bathroom in Nathan's room; she changes into a pair of jogging shorts. An extra-large t-shirt, because of the elastic in the shorts and the shirt is very oversized, they don't tear to shreds when she turns into her aggressive wolf. Still, even she will admit a werewolf wearing a t-shirt and jogging pants cut off into shorts kind of takes away from the intimidation factor. To make sure that she gets the job done right, Aleahcym transforms into her aggressive werewolf form; she moves in close to Nathan and sinks her teeth hard into his upper arm and shoulder. Then in seconds, she becomes human again. She looks over at Caiden and says," now we wait." The infection sets up in Nathans's body quickly; he repeatedly starts to jerk and twist and then lays perfectly still.

Michael decided he stay up and watch since he doesn't sleep anyway. As night fell, Caiden let Michael out of the necklace. Caiden and Aleahcym got some rest. Sometime early the following day, before the sun rose, Michael wakes Caiden, and then he returns to the necklace, and Caiden corks him inside. Aleahcym and Caiden were sitting on a love set that was moved into the room the night before. The timing couldn't have been any worse at noon, lunchtime when everyone inside the nursing home is up and active, and it begins to happen. Nathan's monitors go crazy, beeping and flashing.

Nathan is twisting and jerking and growling. Aleahcym pulls the plug out of the wall to turn off the monitors, and they know a nurse will walk in any second. Caiden goes shadow, runs out the door, and pulls the fire alarm. Then runs back to the room. Aleahcym pulls the privacy curtain around Nathan. Aleacym looks over at Caiden, " you ready, sweetie?" she asked. "Let's do it, " he said. She turns into her timid form, cornering Caiden against the wall, growling and barking at him furiously; just then, the aides burst into the room, "Run," he screams. The aids see the wolf having Caiden cornered and, offering no help, they flea in fear for their lives.

Then Aleahcym, still in wolf form, runs out the door chasing all the aids down the hall. She senses that Nathan's transformation has been complete, and using (were-telepathy), she calms him and commands that he turns human. Nathan immediately complies; instinctively, he knows the voice of his pack leader. Aleahcym makes her way to a bathroom, where she previously stashed a spare set of clothes. Aleahcym bursts into the restroom slips into a stall, then turns human; she pops out the vent in the wall, pulls out a bag with her clothes that she had stashed earlier, and gets dressed. She exits the bathroom and walks back to Nathans's room. After things had calmed down and the fire department cleared the building, they found no fire or wolf. Nathan walked up to the desk and explained who he was. The RN on duty was in disbelief, " I guess with all the commotion, I couldn't sleep anymore," he said And proceeded to collect his belongings and check himself out. They leave the building, climb into the truck and begin the trip home.

Aleahcym lays her hands across her face and screams," STOP!! make em stop," Caiden locks the breaks, and they slide off the road onto the emergency lane of the side interstate. "What is wrong? Stop what?" Caiden asked. She doesn't answer; she sits there and cries. " It's horrible. I can see their faces and feel their fear, and It's too late for me to help them. I could feel them die, everyone, every last one, dead, and all I could do is sit here," she explained. " who died?" I didn't feel or see anything," Nathan said. "The tribe, everyone, and you wouldn't be your only connection to me, and I was born. This way, I must be connected through the bloodline," she said. " I don't know how to tell you this, so I'll just come out and say it, you and I are all that's left of our bloodline. They're all gone, all of them," she said.

Nathan, using were-telepathy, speaks to Aleahcym. "there are only two ways there could be a werewolf outside your pack? one is taking a non-werewolf mate. The second is to infect a human and let them turn; on the upside, now I know my little girl isn't sexually active," Nathan said. " Uh, you guys know we can hear you, right," Caiden said. " how is that possible?" Nathan asked. " Michael's her uncle and a wolf sort-of, and he's hitchhiking off my D.N.A," Caiden said. "Remember me, Nate?" Michael asked. " I do, forgive me, but you and Caiden seem like the same person. Look at you, camo shirt, pants, black trench coat, skull face mask, and then top it all off with a black heart necklace. A nice wardrobe. Is it a Cupid Manson design?" Nathan asked, laughing maniacally. Michael laughs," Man, I've missed you," he said." While I was in limbo for the last eighteen years, I wasn't alone. Asaaluk, Danotta, Emma, and Marla came to me with their knowledge and warnings. Michael, tonight is a lunar eclipse; you need to be over something silver, and you will become flesh at the peak. Then you need to implant something silver into your skin to keep you human, but since it is a lunar eclipse, there isn't any guarantee you can remain human in the daylight, but you will be able to shift at night, human or shadow wolf," Nathan said.

That evening they go to Caiden's house to keep his family safe. Aleahcym and Caiden tell their families how they are madly in love, and they want to elope, go to Alaska, and be in touch. They didn't take it very well, but Caiden's dad believed in his son's ability to make his own decisions, gave his blessing, and told him to keep the truck. It was going to be his for Christmas anyway. After leaving, they went to Jacob's house, and before they could say anything, Jacob told her that he knew this day would soon come. He looks over at Nathan and says," take care of our little girl. She is my daughter too.", " I know and thank you, and I couldn't have raised her better myself," he said, then gave Jacob a firm handshake. Aleahcym collected some of her belongings and said her goodbyes. They load up in the truck and leave.

They decide to drive to a popular scenic overlook on the Blue Ridge Parkway, and there, they will have the best view of the eclipse. They bail out of the truck and stare off into the horizon. It is beautiful to see the bright full moon hanging over the distant city lights. Caiden released Michael from the necklace as the peak of the eclipse approached. Michael takes his place, hovering over top of a silver pocket watch that belonged to Caiden's Grandfather. Then the eclipse peaks and Michael begins to make his transfiguration to human, and he becomes flesh. Caiden takes a silver earring and pushes it through his left earlobe. Caiden picks up his watch and puts it in his pocket. Michael is human again, "Finally, I'm back and hungry after all this time. Please, let's go find some food," said Michael. Everyone laughs aloud.

They loaded back up and went to a local restaurant for a quick meal. Michael noticed something peculiar, the woman sitting a few tables over; every time she lifted her hands to her mouth to take a bite of her burger, he kept seeing a mark on the back of the woman's hand that looked a lot like the same bran burnt behind Aleahcym's ear.

Michael tells Nathan to look over at the woman. Nathan's mouth dropped. After the lady finished eating, she quickly put her gloves back on and went to empty her tray and leave.

Michael determined not to let her leave the parking lot without answering a few questions. So Michael gets up and follows her out. The rest of the crew shortly follow. The lady walks across the parking lot to her car. Michael quickly transforms into the shadow wolf, and like a translucent dark cloud, whooshing across an already darkened background, he darts over in front of her. Then before her eyes, he turns human, "Hi, I think we need to talk," he said. She starts freaking out," How did you find me? Please don't kill me. I was young, I didn't understand," she pleads with Michael. "Whoa, nobody wants to kill you. I just want to ask you, how you got that mark branded on the back of your hand?" Michael explained. The lady grabs Michael's face and turns his head repeatedly in different positions, looking into his eyes, "no asterisked mark, your

not A.K.S? "Oh, think God," she said as she sighed relief.

"A.K.S?" Michael asked. "I don't have to explain anything

to you," She said. Aleahcym walked over to the car, "

please don't be afraid," she said. Then pulled back her hair

and showed the lady the mark behind her ear. The woman's

eye open big as saucers," it's true, you are a wolf?" she

asked. "Well, do you think we could find a place to talk,

and maybe, someplace not so public?" Aleahcym asked. "

I'll make you a deal; you get in the car, we ride and talk,

your shadow stalking friend, babyface, and the old guy,

stay here, and I'll bring you back after," she said. " aw,

come now, I'm not that old," Nathan said. Aleahcym enters

the vehicle, and they drive away.

"My name is Constance," she said. "Aleahcym, nice to

meet you, and yes, this is my answer to your question. I am

a wolf," she said. " Wow, where do I start? I lived in

Canada, and I was a young girl when the Asterisk's Kill

Squad, or A.K.S, came into my home, killed my parents, and took me away to a camp run by evil people who made us do awful things. They burned this symbol into the back of our hands so that we would never forget to kill anyone bearing this symbol behind the ear, no exceptions. There were all types of us, all shifters of all sorts, but no wolves. They trained us to kill you dogs from a very young age." She said. Aleahcm had lots of questions. So Constance Explained all she knew about how A.K.S and they were only interested in shifters, that only passed their abilities through genetics. And all the dogs were impure, turning others outside their bloodline, infecting the world like a plague. So A. K.S was born to rid the world of its impurities." People like us, we are impure, I'm not like you, when A.K.S learned that my kind could infect, with a bite to take on a shifting partner, they killed my people in the camp on the spot, as the example," she explained. "Your kind," said Aleahcym. " My people are in the canine gene pool, but it took two of us to shift, unlike you wolves. We are, what is known to the world as the Cerberus," Constance explained.

"You a three-headed dog?" Aleahcym asked." No, two-headed dog, but I cannot shift because I never took a partner, which helped me escape from them. I had them convinced that the people they killed that night at my house were not my parents but my adopted parents and that I wasn't what they thought I was.

But, because I knew they existed, they would kill me. Then a wolf marked behind her ear like you. She helped me escape and gave her life doing it. Her name was Skylar, and she was my friend. We need to be careful. A.K.S is everywhere, from the typical dog on the street corner, bear in the woods, even a shadow is seen out of the corner of your eye, there are everywhere and nowhere, we cant win this war," she told Aleahcym. "You looked at

Michael's face and said no asterisk. What did you mean?"

said Aleahcym. "A.K.S members are all tattooed, with an

asterisk in the white part of the eye. You only get that mark

once you prove yourself to them.

Once marked, you are a full-fledged A.K.S member

in one of the world's highest re-guarded, secret

organizations, with members as high up as the White

House. I have done my homework, you take that mark, and

your not A.K.S, your entire bloodline vanishes away from

existence," She told Aleahcym. While still driving,

Constance reaches down into the console and pulls up a

contact case. She opens it takes a contact lens, and tries to

put it into her eye. While doing so, she swerves sharply in

the road. Blue lights begin to flash behind them brightly.

She quickly put the contact case back into the console, then

pulled off to the shoulder of the road, and adjusted the

contact lens in her eye. The Officer walked up to her

window," evening Maam, license please" The Police

Officer asked. Then he leans down to peer into her window, takes his flashlight, shines it into the back of the car, and then into Constance's eyes. "Oh, I'm sorry, Mam, for the confusion. Everything is all good here. You ladies have a great night," he said. Then he looks at Constance and winks, and in the bottom corner of his eye is an asterisk tattoo. The Officer walks back to his car. Before he reaches the end of her car, he disappears into thin air, and his partner pulls off.

While at the same time, Constance pulls away and resumes driving," Don't talk. Let me find a place to pull over so that we can talk," she said to Aleahcym. She turns into a well-lit parking lot of a supermarket. "That cop was A.K.S. Why did he look at you and then leave?" she asked. Constance looks over at Aleahcym, and in the bottom corner of her eye is a tattoo of an asterisk. Then Constance reaches to her eye and pulls out the contact lens."I took it out to eat, and you guys stopped me before I could put it back in. No, I'm not A.K.S., that cop was, but I was pretending to be A.K.S. That is the only way to infiltrate their local infrastructure; there is supposed to be a secret training camp somewhere in Independence, Virginia, on a huge farm, but I can't find it, can't even spot it from the air," she said. "Let us help," Aleahcym said. Then Constance takes off and drives down the road a little bit and then pulls back into the parking lot, where Michael, Caiden, and Nathan are. Constance steps out of the car, walks to the trunk, and draws a cell phone from a box. she tosses it to Aleahcym and tells her that she will be in touch. Then she gets back into her car and speeds off.

Aleahcym, curious but cautious, removes the battery from the phone and then gets into the truck and explains the interesting conversation between her and Constance. Then hands the cell phone to Caiden," once every hour, put the battery in and check for missed calls," she said. " Why not just leave it on?" asked Caiden. "I don't trust her yet, and no one needs to keep tabs on our location, tracking the phone's GPS," she said. " OK, dare I will be the one to say it, we need to find a place to call home until tomorrow. I'll make some phone calls and hopefully reinstate my accounts. I guess being asleep for fifteen years or so is the same as being dead, and I need to make a trip to my bank because outside of my accounts, I kept some funds in a safety deposit box, which I think will come in handy now," Nathan told them. " Isn't that in New York?" Aleahcym asked. " Yep," Nathan replied. "Well then, let us drive and sleep in shifts. We can be there in the morning," Caiden said. They all agree, and they load up and are off to New York.

Meanwhile, Constance is back on the interstate heading to her destination, when from behind the back seat rose a dark shadow figure and moves into the front passenger seat.

Then it shifts into human form; it is the police offer that pulled her over earlier and let her go. "Did you miss me?" the officer asked. Constance, extremely startled, swerves across the interstate. Finally, she regains control of the car.

Constance drops her head" you got me," she says. " First, you will call your friends on that phone you gave them. Then, no better yet, you will text them some GPS coordinates for me. That is if my partner hasn't got them yet. Then we will find that secret base you've been looking for, you see, I been hiding back here awhile now. I heard everything, "mmm mmm," he smacks his lips together, making a loud popping sound" I'm going to enjoy breaking you, Missy," he tells her.

Constance pulls off to the shoulder and texts out the coordinates, like she was told, and they switch places so that he can drive. After about an hour's drive, they pull down a long winding gravel road that leads to an old farmhouse and a great big red barn. They pull up to the gated entrance. The man gets out of the car, then walks up to, what looks like an old fence post with a hole bored into it, then he looks into the hole, and a scanner, scans his retina, then the gate opens, he gets back into the car, and that pull up to the house and parks. Something caught her eye; at every corner of the house is a tower, and a giant canvas hangs about 30 feet above the entire house is stretchered across from every tower. They exit the car, and he escorts her to the old-looking, run-down red barn; once at the barn's door, he again looks into a peephole, and like out of an SYFY movie, the perfectly camouflaged metal door slides open very quickly. They enter the barn, and the door quickly closes behind them. Once inside the barn, it was remarkable. It looked like a billion-dollar office building with mutable levels, people, computers, and surveillance equipment everywhere, and it was like walking into the pentagon during wartime. Constance is quickly ushered into an elevator and taken to a secure holding cell underground, where she would later be interrogated. She could hear a conversation in the background, and one particular was a man saying that the vaccine was ready for testing. A man boasts, "Guaranteed to keep a shadow shifter from ever-shifting again."

He then explains that the C.D.C has the vaccine, and tomorrow at 2:00 P.M sharp, it will go under military control. Then she heard him say that he had to get back to Atlanta before being missed. The elevator door closed, and she felt like it dropped thirty stories. She was put in her cell and was amazed that her cell was more like a motel room. It had a private bathroom, a bed, and a mini-fridge stocked with bottled water, but cameras were everywhere, even in the bathroom, she may feel alone, but someone was constantly watching.

The next day Atlanta, Georgia, C.D.C building. Across the parking lot sets a military vehicle with four armed soldiers inside it. A group of casually dressed people, some wearing lab coats, one carrying a briefcase, the others appear to be armed, exit the building and walk toward the military vehicle. The four soldiers step out and walk toward the scientist. Then like a cloud passing in front of the sun, a large shadow moves across the parking lot's pavement, racing toward the scientist. Just as it reaches their feet, four shadow figures pop up from the ground and pass through the scientist; all the scientists fall to the ground, dead. All the shadow figures turn toward the soldiers and toss a shadow object at them. The second the shadow object leaves the shadow figure's hands, it transforms from shadow to a real thing, and four beating hearts smack onto the ground at the soldiers' feet. As fast as lighting, the shadows streaked across the parking lot's pavement and disappeared into the shadows of all the parked cars.

Asterisk's group of shifters returned to her with the vaccine, and she immediately began her testing. The results were fascinating. She found that all shifters who took the vaccine lost their shifting abilities. After some testing, she executed all of her test subjects. Then she turned the vaccine into a virus that's only contracted if ingested. Asterisk calls for a meeting with Enoch. She insists that everyone needs to be present, so they can discuss how and when to deploy their new toy.

The group reaches New York, and Nathan collects his savings and gets all his affairs straightened out at the bank and all his account reinstated. Caiden takes the cell phone that Constance gave them and turns it on, and they receive the text message sent from Constance, but he wasn't sure what to make of it; it looked like a bunch of weird random numbers to him, so he took it to Aleahcym and the rest of the group, and they rack their brains trying to figure it out. Once he heard Nathan say it, he immediately knew that the numbers were coordinates. Through the aid of the internet, the satellite photos turned up nothing except a pond and an old house. So the group decides that they will go check it out,

They all loaded up in the car and began the trip back to Independence, Virginia. Once there, they drive down a gravel road. "Nathan, are you sure these coordinates are right? Aleahcym asked? "Yeah, it should be right around here, somewh....". Before Nathan could finish his sentence, they saw a long line of cars and trucks parked along the roadside and in the field. " I think we found it." Caiden said. Just then, a group of armed men walked up to the car's driver's side window. Nathan rolled down the window when the armed man asked him," are all of you here for the party? "NO," Nathan replies. Then, three other armed guys opened Aleahcym's door and said," Hello wolf, I'm going to need you guys to come with us."

They bring the group inside, where many people sit at tables elegantly set with lots of food and wine. They set the group down at a table beside Enoch and his big group of followers. Enoch notices Aleahcym and the mark behind her ear. He said, "isn't this nice? Asterisk does deliver." he said. At that moment, Enoch stood up. When he did, the room fell quiet "I like to propose a toast to Asterisk and all her efforts to make this day happen' well done, well done indeed." Then Asterisk stands up and curtsy and speaks," Thank you all for coming, please enjoy your meal," and sets back down. Aleahcym, Nathan afraid to eat or drink, Micheal being in the necklace, who can't eat, drink. Caiden looks at his friends and says, "Psalm twenty-three and five." That is all he said, and he began to eat and drink. Aleahcym and Nathan simultaneously say, "Amen." They also eat the food. About ten minutes or so into the meal, Asterisk stand's up with her glass in hand, with a spoon taps the edge of her drink," ding, ding, ding" the room becomes quiet as she speaks, " I would like to show our special guest, a super surprise." Then she shadow shifts along with all her followers, which is about half the room.

Enoch tries to shift but is unable. He is confused. Asterisk gives the command to kill anything that is still human. The slaughter begins, and Aleahcym tries to go werewolf but is unable. Neither is Nathan. But Caiden has no trouble shifting, and Caiden fighting to protect Aleahcym and Nathan but is overwhelmed; while covering Aleahcym, Nathan is brutally ripped apart by a shadow figure. Aleahcym turned to Caiden and said," run " Caiden replied, "No, I'm not leaving you" "Run now," she shouted! Tears fill Caidens eye's he knows he can't protect her much longer. There are just too many of them. Aleahcym can see the shadow figures coming toward her. Bracing for sudden death, she closes her eyes; peace overtakes her, Then with the force of a being hit by a truck. A shadow shifter hits her from behind. She stands there in shock as his arm trusts, through her back and out of her cheat raising her off her feet off the ground, her body goes limp, and when it lets her go, she collapses to the floor.

Aleahcym lay on the floor dying, and this is when she realizes her full potential; all is dark now, as her mind begins to search the void, then like tiny dots of lights popping up out of the darkness, looking like small far off galaxies if the distant black nothingness. She looks closer at one of them, and as she does, she can see the lives of people flashing before her eyes at light speed, as if they were her memories. Then at this exact point in time, the Dragon, named Darkness, who guards the void, can now see Aleahcym in his mind's eye. He now knows her location, then races off into the darkness to kill her. Aleahcym's mind stops on a vision of Asaaluk standing bound in front of a fire. She reaches out and touches the light. Suddenly, Aleahcym's thoughts and memories are shared with Asaaluk, then Aleahcym's body, which lay dying on the floor, instantly turns to ash.

Alec is at the center of the village, stoking a reasonably good size fire. He is making sure he gets the branding iron cherry red for Asaaluk and enjoys every second of it. Several members of Alec's tribe have suggested to him that he should just let it go. She has served her time and suffered enough. Alec spits at them and then reminds them that it wasn't their son or wife who was killed. Now all the members of both tribes are gathering at the center of the village, and there is a lot of muttering amongst them. Then Asaaluk is brought to the center, her hands bound. She stands before them in a trans-like state, and silence falls over the crowd; they are shocked to see that Asaaluk is pregnant. Then you can hear a child screaming among all the people, and it's Enoch. His sitter is frantically trying to get him to stop.

Asaaluk stands in front of Alec with a cold, dark emptiness in her eyes. Alec looks over at Asaaluk and smirks as he reaches for the branding iron. Then, as if time is frozen, Asaaluk breaks her restraints, reaches up, grabs her ear with the silver bit embedded in it, and rips her ear off the side of her face; simultaneously. She lunges at Alec. While her other arm punches at him, and in mid punch, she turns werewolf, and her fist runs clean through his chest. She drops his heart out of his back, and in that instant, she does a backflip into the crowd. Just before her feet hit the ground in mid-flight, she has taken little Enoch away from his sitter. With her right hand, she grabs the top of his little head and twists, popping his tiny head off his body, then she takes three steps back, placing her and what's left of Enoch into the center of the fire, and while burning she changes back into her human form. Then almost like magic, their bodies quickly turn into ash and fall to the ground with force so great it put out the fire. The tribes' people are looking at the orange glow under the pile of ashes. The wind begins to pick up, but only at the ashes, the orange glow becomes brighter, and the ashes begin to form an ash-like image of a small girl wearing a long hooded robe. She raises her hands toward the tribe's people, and in a loud voice, as if it were thunder, she says," The darkness comes here!" "Then the Dragon called Darkness swoops down from the sky, opens its mouth, and spits a thick black dark fog, covering the whole area all the other people and me, and then everything went black, and that is when I woke up," Mychaela said. "Mychaela, I will count backward from 3 to 1; when I reach one, you will awake alert and refreshed and remember everything we have talked about, three, two, one," said Dr. Jennings. " So, let me guess? You think I'm crazy! Right?" said Mychaela. "No, in my professional opinion, you're stressed. I assure you that you are not part of an ancient Alaskan werewolf tribe." She said. She adds."You are experiencing a form of lucid dreams, not memories." Mychaela sets up on the sofa and exclaims! " They're not dreams!" "Mychaela, sweety, it is all metaphors. Let me break it down for you. For example, you told me last week you wrote a six-page essay on secret societies and the shifters and werewolves. I believe they represent society as a whole. The void is anything that might keep you from achieving your main goals in life. The Dragon is the thief, and even the Bible says the thief came to kill, steal and destroy. I have explained away all this nonsense in just a few sentences." Said Dr. Jennings.

"I want you to take it easy this week, go have some fun relax; I'll prescribe something to help you sleep. Then, come back and see me in one month." Said Dr. Jennnings. Mychaela gets off the sofa, adjusts her camouflage skirt, straightens her black onyx heart-shaped necklace, pulls up her skull face bandana above her nose, walks to the door, exits, and gently closes the door behind her.

My Testimony

When I first came to Christ, I was twelve and gave my heart to the Lord. We lived in an apartment complex about two miles from a baptist church, which would run a bus and pick my brother and me up along with some other neighborhood children who lived in the same complex. I guess we went there on and off for about three years. But we eventually moved out of town way back in the middle of nowhere, and I didn't go to church for a while. I did go to some churches on and off but fell away. After I graduated, I got mixed up in the dark world of drugs and alcohol; it seemed to start on the weekends as a social activity but became a habit. I met my wife when I was twenty-five (who didn't drink or do drugs). We met a work, dated for about three months, then decided to get married. So I'm now twenty-six years old, married, and about two weeks away from being a daddy for the first time. It was about 5:30 one evening in March of 2000. I kissed my wife, I loaded up into the car, and I was off, on my way to join a local lodge, a drinking lodge. I was going to pledge my life to drink. Ok, so this is the part where I say BUT- GOD. Because God had other plans for me, As I am driving down the road at roughly sixty miles an hour, a car fails to the stop sign at the end of his road. I sped up and moved to the other lane facing oncoming traffic to avoid an accident, but it was too late, and I got hit in the back passenger tire. The tire blows, sending my car into a barrel roll. Just as my car began to flip for the first time, I prayed and repented. I knew I wouldn't make it out of this one, and I was traveling at about seventy miles an hour when I got hit. I was not wearing a set belt. I said, "God, please forgive me for my sins." Bang," the sound of the car smashing onto the road; just before that sound, it was like a weight on my chest forcing me back against my seat as my car goes through a series of rolls. After it was over and my car stopped, I jumped out, and I was in disbelief. I had survived the crash with nothing but a bruise on my arm. I lived to see my child be born, not just one but also two others. I have three exceptional children.

I have been clean from drugs now. I believe nineteen years, no alcohol in nine years, and tobacco-free for eight. I remember when I was trying to quit smoking. I tried and failed. I got tired of trying and even told God I wouldn't try anymore. If I wasn't supposed to smoke, I guessed he

would have to take it because I'm not going to try and quit anymore. About a year after that prayer, I watched my dad fight lung cancer. One night I got sick, coughing and gagging, coughing some more. I coughed up blood, and I thought wow this is just great, I have been watching my dad go through his first fight with lung cancer, and now I'm going to do this to my family, My wife took me to the (E.R.) and I explained all my symptoms to the Doctor on call. He told us upfront he thought it was throat cancer and ordered an M.R.I . Do you know how much praying you can do when you pray for your life? Do you know that God is faithful? It turned out it was a major sinus infection, not cancer, but guess what? I Never touched another cigarette from that night forward. On a sad note, my dad (Edcel Noah Paschall) lost his battle on April 14, 2018, and I miss him dearly. God has led me to The Rock Worship Center, where I currently serve on the media team. Through God, I have also founded prayerknight.com as a way for me to help reach the lost and spread to Gospel of Jesus Christ.
Brian Paschall 11/08/2021